A Much-Married Man

A Novel

BOOKS BY ROBERT SWARD

POETRY

❖ *Advertisements*, Odyssey Chapbook Number One, 1958
❖ *Uncle Dog & Other Poems*, 1962
❖ *Kissing The Dancer & Other Poems*,
   Introduction by William Meredith, 1964
❖ *Thousand-Year-Old Fiancee*, 1965
❖ *Horgbortom Stringbottom, I Am Yours, You Are History*, 1970
❖ *Hannah's Cartoon*, 1970
❖ *Quorum/Noah* (With Mike Doyle), 1970
❖ *Gift*, 1971
❖ *Five Iowa Poems*, 1975
❖ *Cheers For Muktananda*, 1976
❖ *Honey Bear On Lasqueti Island, B.C.*, 1978
❖ *Six Poems*, 1980
❖ *Twelve Poems*, 1982
❖ *Movies: Left To Right*, 1983
❖ *Half-A-Life's History, Poems New & Selected*,
   Introduction by Earle Birney, 1983
❖ *The Three Roberts, Premiere Performance*, 1984
   (Featuring Robert Priest, Robert Zend, and Robert Sward)
❖ *The Three Roberts On Love*, 1985
❖ *The Three Roberts On Childhood*, 1985
❖ *Poet Santa Cruz*, Introduction by Morton Marcus, 1985
❖ *Four Incarnations: New & Selected Poems* (1957-1991), 1991
❖ *Family* (with David Swanger, Tilly Shaw & Charles Atkinson), 1994

FICTION

❖ *The Jurassic Shales*, A Novel, 1975

NON-FICTION

❖ *The Toronto Islands*, An Illustrated History, 1983

EDITED BY ROBERT SWARD

❖ *Vancouver Island Poems*, An Anthology, 1973
❖ *Emily Carr: The Untold Story*, 1978

A Much-Married Man

A Novel

Robert Sward

Ekstasis Editions

Canadian Cataloguing in Publication Data

Sward, Robert, 1933
      A much-married man
      Novel.
      ISBN 0-921215-99-1
      I. Title.
      PS 8587.W35M82 1996   C813.54
      PR 9199.3.S94M82 1996   C96-910120-1

Cover art: Noreen Tomlinson, "What Will the Neighbours Say?"
Author photo: Paul Schraub

Acknowledgments: Portions of this work were originally published in different form in *Ambit Magazine* (London, England), *Blue Penny Quarterly* (Internet), *CrossConnect* (University of Pennsylvania), *eSCENE* (Internet), *Gruene Street* (Internet), *Hawk* (Internet), *The Toronto Star* (Canada), *Monterey Life Magazine*, *rpoetik* (Internet), *The San Jose Mercury News*, and *Zero City* (Internet). Grateful acknowledgment is made to the editors of these publications.

A Much-Married Man has been published with the assistance of a grant from the Canada Council and the Cultural Services Branch of British Columbia.

Ekstasis Editions Canada Ltd.   **Ekstasis Editions**
Box 8474, Main Postal Outlet   Box 571
Victoria, B.C. V8W 3S1   Banff, Alberta TOL OCO

Gloria in Excelsis

With special thanks to
Charles Atkinson, Dion Farquhar, Joan Friedland,
William Minor, David Swanger and Tilly Shaw.

O Heavenly muse
unfold the wanderer's tale.
Commence, lady,
at whichever scene you will.
—The Odyssey

The present is the only thing that has no end.
—Schrodinger

A man who desires to get married should know
either everything or nothing.
—Oscar Wilde

Yet there is a mystery here and it is not one
that I understand: without this sting of otherness,
of—even—the vicious, without the terrible energies
of the underside of health, sanity, sense,
then nothing works or can work. I tell you that goodness
—what we in our ordinary daylight selves call goodness:
the ordinary, the decent—
these are nothing without the hidden powers
that pour forth continually from their shadow sides.
—Doris Lessing

1

A Habit Worse Than Heroin

It takes several lives to make one person.

—Carlos Fuentes

Mt. Chakra, The Santa Cruz Mountains

DECEMBER 22

First he puts on his blue fleece-lined sweat pants and thickly padded shirt. Then he pulls on the loose red polyester pants and calf-length acrylic socks (one size fits all). He steps into his high rubber boots with the white rabbit fur and, car keys in hand, red wrinkle-free Santa jacket over his arm, pauses to check himself in the bathroom mirror.

"Head up, back straight..." He can hear her now, Miss Chicago, his ex-beauty queen mother. "You've got to watch your posture. Keep that chin in. That's it. That's it. Stand tall. Remember to smile, darling. You're a serious fellow. You've got good genes. You should be pleased with your looks."

"Forget it, Mom, for Godsake."

"Listen to me. I know what I'm talking about," she'd say, tilting her head back and looking him in the eye.

That was two years before she died. At thirteen, Noah stood 6'1", weighed 145 pounds and, a marksman-like pitcher, was being courted by high school coaches. He was also the son of a bourbon-loving borscht belt comedian. For her part, Miss Chicago was doing all she could to build his confidence.

He checks the features she once praised him for, full lips, rosy cheeks and hazel brown "bedroom eyes." Unreal face. How can he look one way and feel another? He feels like a clone of himself. How many Noah Newmarks are there? He runs a hand through his reddish hair, each curl resembling a question mark. Why did Holly leave? "Marriage is the hog butcher of love," she once hollered. Being married to her…was that what did the marriage in? His neck and jaw tighten. Again, he does as the beauty queen taught him to do. He notices what in his body needs attention and speaks to those parts. "Jaw, unclench. Neck, loosen. Eyes, stop squinting."

How responsible are we for our faces?

"After thirty-five," Shelley Levine liked to say, "our faces are ourselves. That's where people can see how we've lived our lives."

"That sounds like something from *Bartlett's Familiar Quotations*," he'd joked.

"Who said it doesn't matter. What I want to know is: do you agree or not?"

"Shelley, honey, you're right." Shelley Levine. Wife #1.

At 47, he's a chivalrous standard-bearer in Cupid's army, a veteran of five shots at bliss. Divorce suits, court appearances, child custody cases, alimony, support payments, nothing served to dampen his ardor. Of course each shot at bliss, each dissolution, left him in need of healing. In Noah's case, recovery took two to three years. But then, having paid up, having made amends, and, typically with the blessings of all concerned, the word *Amor!* on his lips, the banner of love flapping in the breeze, he'd ride off again on a quest for the beloved.

O sweetest joy, O light from heaven, O wildest woe… He recalls the line from a book he bought while courting his first wife.

Now he's aging. Something's off. Tanned, clear skin taut over high cheekbones. Thick eyebrows and long eyelashes his wives teased him about and claimed to envy. A serviceable face marred lately by puffy eyes. A bearded but guileless face that, at this moment, looks back at him with a haunted cast to it. What's off, he decides, is he looks bemused, befuddled–stupid. Five wives and four children and he hasn't learned anything and it shows. *Dumkopf!*

This time, he decides, he's going to fight to stay married. This time, the banner of love snapping in the breeze, he'll ride off in quest of the wife he refuses to lose. Fuck divorce. Hail love, honor and fidelity. Hail respect for one's partner. Fuck dissolution. Hail remembering why one got married in the first place. Infidelity is for infidels.

Noah adjusts the Santa cap. He runs his fingers through his red beard. He'll attach the Santa beard later.

"Sonofabitch. Is this how I want to spend my life? A Rent-A-Hack. Playing games. Asking questions I already know the answers to." The door bangs shut behind him.

Hunter Thompson was right. *Writing's a habit worse than heroin.* He picks up a chunk of firewood and hurls it at the bedroom window. When he hears the window explode, Noah dances in the roadway.

Of course. One way or another he'll pay for it.

Gonzo journalism. Bullshit! What does the word mean? The word *Gonzo* means simpleton. Macho simpleton. Noah feels like a simpleton.

He climbs into the chalky green Volvo and rolls up the windows, turns on the air conditioner. Six-foot, blond, blue-eyed, red-cheeked, gap-toothed Mrs. Claus was supposed to be here to say goodbye each time he set out on a gig. That was the idea, wasn't it? Only she set him up to make her getaway. Set him up, too, to grab Joey out of Mt. Chakra's children's dorm. But why?

Bored. That's why Holly left. Wife #5 was bored with Mt. Chakra. Bored with Noah's 12-hours-a-day work routine. Bored with his note-taking and obsession with language. Bored with tofu, cottage cheese and the teachings of Rama P. Rama.

The Wise One. Where was the "wise one" on this one?

Holly's a TV daytime soap star forever struggling to memo-rize lines and lose another two or three pounds. Non-fat this and non-fat that. Grapefruit, grapefruit, grapefruit. And her with an appetite too for diamonds, dry champagne, and any and all hours of the day, fall-out-of-bed, acrobatic sex. Miss Inexhaustible Energy (her showbiz nickname), queenly Penelope of *My Many Children*. What was Noah thinking?

"It'll be a chance to get out of Los Angeles, lose five pounds and get my shit in order. And I won't have to wear industrial strength make-up either. Ah, fresh air. We can hike and camp and screw in a hammock. The pure life!"

That's how she agreed to spend the holidays—all expenses paid, V.I.P. lodgings—at Mt. Chakra.

Now he'd have to wrap up the *Our Times Magazine* article—double time—and take off after her.

Goodbye vegetarian rice and beans. Goodbye picture post-card mountain view. Meditation at 6:00 A.M. The Sun Salutation and the Cobra by dawn's early light and thinking that he might not only fulfill an assignment, but resuscitate a marriage.

Goddamnit, if yoga means union, means to bring together darkness and light; love-flesh and life-breath; Eros and Psyche; mortality and immortality; the yoking together of Blip and Blop, then it stood to be the means by which Holly Hollander and Noah Newmark might re-unite.

But he never talked to her, never spoke of his vision, of how, different as their lives had become—her twelve-hour days on the set, his twelve-hour days on a story—they might re-wed, re-mate, reconstitute their marriage.

So, instead, he says goodbye. Goodbye realignment, goodbye marital overhaul, marital restoration, marital makeover.

Goodbye yogis and yogi aficionados.

Goodbye vegetarian volleyball and pickup baseball games.

Goodbye? Goodbye nothing. Fuck goodbye! I'll win her back. Whatever it takes, I'll pay the price.

He turns the key, sets the Volvo speed control at a manly 70 miles per hour and heads for Highway 17.

2

How to Cure a Broken Heart

Highway 17, The Santa Cruz Mountains

W hat is the cure? What is the cure for a broken heart?" he asks, speaking into a voice-activated tape recorder. "Okay, so I'm obsessed. So I'm addicted to writing–and to teaching writing. Not easy to live with. So what? So what's the problem?" He punches one hand into the other. "Anyway, how about a feature? A dozen interviews with photos. Re-check the stats, write up the results. A new take on the old story.

> FACT: Four out of every five people who have been divorced want to re-marry, and often do re-marry—someone much like their former spouse.
>
> FACT: Three of every ten marriages involve people for whom the first try did not work.
>
> QUESTION: Why do people re-marry? How, after a hellish, crazy-making divorce, do they manage to recover to the point that they can risk—again?
>
> LEAD: "Want to cure a broken heart? Try re-marriage. It's a fact: three out of every ten marriages involve people for whom the first try did not work. Why do they re-marry?"

He pitches the story, sounds it out, sells himself on the idea, driving all the while over mountainous Highway 17, bumper-to-bumper with 17,000 commuters, past the turnoff to Scott's Valley, past Borland's computer factory, defunct Santa's Village, past Summit Inn and Cloud 9 Trading Post. Spicy smelling, drought-stricken eucalyptus trees. Bare hillsides looking as if they'd been strip-mined. A smoky haze over the charred mountains. Redwoods. Douglas fir. Paramedics. Ambulances. The stench of burning rubber.

Creeping along at twenty miles an hour, Santa removes his cap, unbuttons the red jacket and wipes sweat from his forehead. Unable to get the air conditioner to work, he punches the dashboard. Wheezing, he turns on the car radio and listens to his favorite morning show, *Disaster Up-Date.*

"Five years of drought, a fire, and a massive earthquake. This is God's country? The only precedents for what we've faced are biblical. As a spokesperson for the governor says, 'We're running three plagues behind Egypt.' But be assured, the California Dream is still alive—even if it means living elbow to elbow with one's neighbor on a brushy hillside.

"Now, back to Johnny Gillespie at *Sound Salad.* Remember to stay tuned for *Dynaflow Diner* at noon and *Continental Drift* at one o'clock."

Santa turns next to Dr. Alarm Clock and his *Techno-Muzak Wake-Up Hour.* Muzak for the 21st Century. That's followed by *Talking Classifieds*, New Age announcements read by Natalie Kravitz. She teaches in Santa Cruz and has a Ph.D. in Psychology—of the Inner Child. "We all have an inner child who is begging to be heard," she says. "Won't you become one with that inner child and let her out to play?"

Noah presses a button to roll down the electric window. He's fortunate. Not having eaten breakfast, he has no breakfast to lose.

Dr. Kravitz invites her listeners to attend her *Uncoupling Group,* a weekly discussion for people who have recently experienced the end of an intimate relationship.

Noah considers attending one of Dr. Kravitz' Uncoupling Groups as a discussion leader. Ambling into a classroom at the Louden Nelson Community Center and, dressed as Saint Nick, standing beside a rickety, old folding chair to tell all he knows about uncoupling. "My name is Noah Newmark, and I've been married five times. I am here to share what I know about divorce. Of course the word *divorce* is technically incorrect. As you know, in California marriages are dissolved and one gets a dissolution, not a divorce. Each year approximately 150,000 Petitions for Dissolution are filed in California.

"*Dissolution*. Think about it for a moment. If something dissolves, it isn't there anymore. Or, you might say, it turns to liquid and you just flush it away. It's the California fresh start. The new life. Get a dissolution and re-invent yourself.

Noah thinks better of it. "An Uncoupling Group. Not likely," he growls. "Dissolution may be my specialty, but I don't have to lecture on dissolution." Besides, fantasies of becoming a crazed, flesh-eating terrier, biting and shaking Holly, alternate with dreams of how they might get back together. Images of reconciliation alternate with images of lawyers and an old-fashioned divorce court. Who was it who said, *You know nothing of a woman until you meet her in court?*

Noah prays her leaving is not the end.

> *Dear God. The Lord is my shepherd; I shall not want... You're there, aren't you God? Okay, then please tell me: do you want me to follow the bitch, beg her to come back? I'll do it. It's Holly or no one. And you're against divorce, and I know it's hypocritical of me to say this, but I'm against divorce too.*

Noah listens as Dr. Kravitz recommends a "Recession Special. Intuitive, deep tissue, Swedish massage and acupressure. Two one-hour sessions for $75. Call Bobbi Congress. Ask about

Bobbi's whole body massage. Comfortable surroundings. Evenings and weekends."

Seventy-five dollars? Noah would willingly spend twice that to be touched. Hearing the word *Congress*, he pushes himself to see if he can feel some sexual stirring. Wants to rub his face in it, wants to punish himself for all the times he used sex to blunt the pain. "A man's wife leaves and normal, he says, poking himself in the head, normal would be to hide out, to have nothing to do with women for a while.

"But not you, Newmark. What would it take for you to be done with this bullshit? What would it be like to be alone for a while?"

Shifting gears, accelerating, half way into the passing lane, he sees an old Dodge which refuses to be overtaken.

Rear-ended, he loses control, spins around and ends up on the side of the road, the sound of honking in his ears. The Dodge, picking up speed, disappears in the distance.

"Welcome to Calamity Road," someone yells a moment later as he stands on the shoulder waving for help.

Turning to the cement road divider, he picks out the action scratches—hieroglyphics of Volvo on concrete.

He checks his Day-Timer. At exactly 11:00 A.M., he's scheduled to mount the throne at Terry the Trickster's Toy Store in San Jose and cry, "Ho ho ho." Once installed, he'll play the King of Hearts, Gift-Bringer to several hundred children. And then write the inside story on how he got the job and his adventures as a Jewish Santa.

Then back to Mt. Chakra for his interview with the Champion of Living, the silent one.

There are afterimages that won't go away. Stock footage of those first horrific hours—dream-state numbness, grief and rage.

The re-appearance of ghosts from marriages past. Shelley Levine. Anna Jones. Dolores Divine. Natasha Kaminsky. And now Holly. And of course the children, Joey, Ariel, Jim and Carol. Mothers-in-law. Fathers-in-law. Sisters-in-law. Brothers-in-law. What a trail he's left.

Dazed, head throbbing, Noah slides back into the driver's seat, and turns the ignition key. The engine chatters, pulls into the line of traffic and stalls behind a truck loaded with chickens, itself stalled behind Seaside Refrigeration.

He opens the door and steps out onto the highway.

"What's going on?" asks a young woman in the next lane.

"Radio says there's an accident," answers Seaside Refrigeration. *"We could be here all day. You want a chocolate chip cookie, lady? Yeah. Here, I've got some coffee too. Yeah, yeah, there's a thermos in the truck. Help yourself."*

"I gotta pee, Momma."

"Ok, ok, Shane. Go in the bushes. Over there."

"I'm scared."

"Everyone else is doing it."

Often, when he is under stress, Noah pounds on the roof of his car. Other times he focuses on some charged word, any word, and his mind fills with all the associations that word has for him. He also spouts dictionary definitions, facts, end-of-column items and oddball statistics. It occurs to him that if he were under enough stress, his mind might turn into something resembling *Roget's Thesaurus.*

Is this strange? Is this unnatural? The son of a former Hebrew teacher—and stand-up comedian—Noah came to believe that looking up works in the dictionary was a form of prayer. He can remember how, as an eight-year-old, each time he looked up a word in the dictionary, his mother or father rewarded him with a teaspoon of honey or a bite of halvah.

"Noah, darling, remember: naming is the glue which holds the world together," said his father in that sing-song, Jackie Mason voice of his, the sorrowful voice of the Jewish liturgical tradition. Like father, like son.

Noah had just turned fifteen when his mother crashed the car, marking an end to the days of halvah and honey, an end to whatever glue it was that held the world together. Before her death, at the Sabbath meal, his mother lit the candles and his father gave him his blessing. Wearing his trademark red V-neck sweater, David Newmark would place his hands on Noah's head and recite the benediction.

"May the Lord bless you and keep you. May He send His light into your life and deal graciously with you. May He look favorably upon you and grant you *shalom,* peace."

Soon after she died, Noah's borscht belt father, back from a gig, the smell of whiskey on his breath, punched him in the head for no reason. "Unfairness has to start early," he explained. "And don't you make me feel guilty by crying. I won't have that. I won't have a son of mine blubbering away at the dinner table. Here, here's a handkerchief. Listen to me now: the world is unfair. Some good-byes are more terminal than others. Our notion that we have control is *meshugga,* crazy. We say, God wouldn't send anything I couldn't bear. That's *meshugga.*

"God Himself is *meshugga.* Take his love of Abraham in the Bible. Why should He love Abraham more than someone else and then ask Abraham to slaughter his son?

"And God's love of the Jews, what is that if not *meshugga?*"

Meshugga. Not having said good-bye to her, his Dead-On-Arrival mother, Noah grieved for years. And his father, though he went on traveling and performing, went on telling jokes, never spoke of her again.

After his mother's death, Noah would periodically charge into the high school locker room, arms swinging, attacking a group of five or more of his toughest classmates. *Alle yevonim hoben ayn ponim,* "all brutes have the same face," he'd cry, pounding with his fists on the undifferentiated mass of bodies.

Sometimes he'd hallucinate. He'd see his dead mother present, however briefly, in the bodies of 15- and 16-year-old boys. Frightened, fearful of losing his mind, he'd go on punching. What if he were pounding not only on their bodies, but on her body? Well, fuck it, he thought. She must have somehow chosen to die and she deserves what she gets. Punching out his classmates seemed as good a way as any to break with her, to say goodbye to her.

In his blind flailing, he was as likely to strike a Jew as a *goy.* He didn't discriminate. He'd simply curse the others for being "other," curse his kicking and punching high school buddies for whatever membrane of difference he felt separated him from them.

In Noah's kamikaze moments, the will to strike with his elbows and fists combined with the longing to merge his body with their bodies, his heart with their hearts. At such times, whatever grief, whatever madness he felt erupted—or was transformed—into joyous rage. Of course he knew he was not about to merge with anyone. He just felt ready to pound on his classmates and, willing to pay the price, he let loose. Thus, bloodied or not in these encounters, Noah found them, on the whole, warmly satisfying.

Bruised, cleansed, laughing, ecstatic, Noah knew joy, joy which, be it confessed, he had never known while his mother was alive.

Officials at Lincoln High expressed concern.

Mr. Marsh, the principal, called Noah into his office and threatened him with expulsion. "You're telling me that you attack your schoolmates to test the rules? Is that right, Noah?" asked Mr. Marsh.

"Yes, sir. I like it when they fight back."

At last, unable to believe that the polite, bespectacled scholar-athlete would mount unprovoked attacks on known *terrorists,* Mr. Marsh simply shook his head and smiled. Perhaps he believed Noah was deliberately taking the blame in order to protect the true troublemakers.

The traffic begins moving. Then stops. Moves. Stops again. Noah turns up the volume and hears Dr. Kravitz recommend a free support group "for people whose pets have died or been lost in some other way. Call for more information about Pet Loss Grief Support. And remember, dear ones, don't let another day go by without tuning in to your inner child."

Enough. Noah switches stations.

Citing Tom Parker's book, *In One Day,* the news reader says, "each day 50,000 people buy new television sets, and 200 Americans have their breasts enlarged, 90 have their breasts reduced, and a total of 35 have their breasts lifted or aimed in some other direction.

"There are 10,000,000 more Americans now than there were five years ago and most of them own cars and spend their free time driving to San Jose and back on Highway 17."

Noah takes off his sunglasses. Turns the dial. A husky-voiced psychic, aura reader and healer from Los Angeles is trying to drum up interest in her $300 weekend seminar, *How To Cure A Broken Heart.*

"My name is Dr. Feingold," says the woman. "Dr. Felicia K.

Feingold from Love Connection Clinic. Yes, that's right, the Doctor of Love herself. Also known as Dr. Permission. Friends, I give you permission, I give you permission ONE AND ALL— RIGHT NOW—to make your connection to the Love Connection. Call now to attend *How To Cure A Broken Heart*. "You've heard of me, haven't you? Of course you have. I'm up here today in the Bay Area from El Lay, ha ha, what you folks in Northern California call Lala Land. I have a question about the human heart. Listeners, honestly, did you know women have two hearts? Yes, you heard me right. Women have two hearts. Women are double hearted. That's the honest to God truth. Tell me, how can that be?"

Noah doesn't know the answer. Two hearts? He knows he has one heart in his chest beating 120 times a minute. He knows that most men's testicles churn out sperm at the prodigious rate of 1,000 per second—30 billion sperm a year.

"Well, numbers aren't everything," he says aloud.

Inhaling diesel exhaust, creeping along now at 15 miles an hour behind a cement truck with a bumper sticker declaring ESCHEW OBFUSCATION, Noah is startled to hear Dr. Feingold remark, "Women are superior to men. Women outlive men. Women have more gusto, more of an appetite for sex than men. Women are more intuitive, more compassionate. Women are the birth givers. Women are the creators. Women are the destroyers."

"Oh, come on, lady." Noah shifts down into first. Seeing an opening, he steps on the accelerator. Shifts back into second, hits the horn, passes the cement truck. Traffic comes to a stop. Noah's stuck behind a garbage truck. Ecologically sound, politically correct, its bumper sticker reads SAVE A TREE—VOICE MAIL IS REAL.

The Volvo overheats. He pulls out his spiral notebook.

An aficionado of bumper stickers, he writes *Save a tree...* The engine dies. Helicopters hover overhead. In the opposite lane Santa sees a small white van filled with a dozen or so dogs, recruits, no doubt, for a s.p.c.a. Christmas giveaway. Like his Volvo, the van of dogs is stopped in traffic. Santa rolls down his window and, looking into the eyes of the terror-stricken canines, he throws back his head, howls in sympathy. "Woooowwwwwll."

"Hey, you, re-taRRd," he hears someone laugh.

Catching Noah's eye, the s.p.c.a driver grins before displaying a slightly drooly, open mouth. The man has no neck and his linebacker shoulders appear to be a direct extension of the lower part of his face. "Duhhhh," he says, pointing at his left ear. Then, with his forefinger, he makes a series of four concentric circles around that ear.

"Hey, jerko Santa Claus! Go back to Santa Cruz where you belong," he sneers.

Responding in kind, Noah displays his left middle finger in the vertical position.

The s.p.c.a driver changes color and begins pounding on his horn. He swivels as if ready to get out of his vehicle and charge, the dogs all barking in unison.

Luckily for Noah, the traffic starts moving.

Catching the driver's eye, Noah shouts, "And a merry Christmas to you, you ape-neck dork."

Braking, jumping out of his vehicle with a dog net, the driver heads for Noah's Volvo.

One of the van's occupants, a German shepherd, glances at Noah with concern.

Blinking his lights, waving at the dog, Noah hits the accelerator and makes good his escape.

He drives twenty feet. Stops. Starts. Stops. Starts and sees a flashing red light in his rear view mirror.

"Whew! Well, it ain't me, babe," he sings, turning up the volume.

The Doctor of Love continues. "The heart is the only organ in a man's body with smooth muscle tissue. A woman's heart is made with smooth muscle tissue, but so is her uterus. So there you are. Women have two hearts. Men have only one."

It's then he hears the siren, *Awwr,* and sees Hell's Angels bikers and cars scattering left and right.

Pulling alongside the Volvo, the cop signals Noah to turn onto the emergency lane.

In no hurry to approach, the highway patrolman sits in his car speaking into a microphone.

Noah stays tuned to Felicia Feingold, but turns off the ignition.

"Now, the good news is that marriages are temporary. The bad news is that ex-husbands are forever. The good news is that you don't have to take it anymore. The bad news is you need money to be free."

Noah recalls Dr. Rama P. Rama's teaching: MARRIAGE IS ETER-NAL. DIVORCE OR NO DIVORCE, YOU ARE BOUND TO YOUR SPOUSES, ALL YOUR SPOUSES AND ALL YOUR CHILDREN, FOR ALL TIME. THE CONNECTION CONTIN-UES INTO THE NEXT LIFE.

Sporting wrap-around sunglasses and a tiny mustache, the cop steps out of his car. Hand on his holster, he motions for Noah to roll down the window.

"What's the matter, you drunk or something? I saw you back there. Did you know you were driving erratically?"

"No, officer, I didn't."

"Lemme see your driver's license and registration."

Noah produces the documents.

"Okay," says the cop, "step out of the car. And take off that cap! That's it. Now, hands at your sides, heel of your left foot touching the toes of your right foot, I want you to walk that white line there until I say stop."

Maintaining his balance, Noah does as he is told.

"Do you live around here?"

"Santa Cruz Mountains," he answers, "Mt. Chakra."

"Ah, that explains it," says the cop, glancing at Noah's beard. "Where you headed?"

"San Jose. I'm scheduled to do a gig. I'm a Rent-A-Santa."

"A Rent-A-what?"

"I'm a Rent-A-Santa. I work a job or two in one place, and then go on to another," says Noah.

"Hmm. One unsafe door, headlights broken...and driving too slowly and erratically," says the cop, writing up the ticket.

"Slowly? Of course I'm going slowly. What do you do in bumper to bumper traffic?"

"Next time just forget the car," he says, thrusting the ticket into Noah's hand. "Use your reindeer."

Noah glances at the sky at what appears to be a belated sunrise, a sunrise he can smell, that burns his throat, an itchy, sweet-tasting, eye-stinging, pinkish-white blanket of smog.

He drives another fifty feet and again the traffic stops. He opens his notebook. He's a writer. Writers write.

> Madrone, arbutus, rock slide, redbark salmon-colored moonscape...earthquake hillside tumbleweed...
>
> At the corner of Truck Turnoff and Winding Road Next 8 Miles, warning flares signal a new day.
>
> Rise and shine, semiconducting devices. Good morning, hard drives. Ah, sweet-smelling, Silicon Valley atomic-power equipment plants.

Dr. F. starts again. "I know you're out there and I know you're grieving for someone dear to you. You're angry, you hurt and you're doing things to hurt yourself. 'No one cares,' you say. But—*pause*—I care."

"What? Who said that? O God, she's just fishing. It's a gimmick."

"Have faith. You know who I'm talking to. I know you're there. It's true you cannot mend a broken heart, but you can grow a new one. Take some time off. What do you need most at this time in your life?"

"What do I need? I need to really look at my life. I need Holly to come home. I need to be okay if Holly doesn't come home. I need to find out what I'm doing with my life, and not masquerade as a devotee of marriage when I'm a devotee of separation. I've got a son and daughter I don't know. Jim and Carol both have jobs—Carol the actress, Jim the photographer— and are getting ready to marry and have children. How can I know them? The only time I see them is when I'm passing through on assignment for some magazine. I phone ahead ('Hello, Jim? Carol? I'll be at the airport—between flights—for a couple hours. Can we meet for dinner?')."

Fucking sterile airports. Meeting kids on neutral ground has its uses. He loves his children, but Holly calls him a marriage glutton, a hit-and-run father. She's right. How close can a five-times married man be to five families? Here today. Gone tomorrow. The journalist, assignment-obsessed father pounding out stories at 30,000 feet. Taking off and landing. Taking off and landing.

Excuses, excuses. He's good at excuses.

The truth is it's easier to keep a distance. Easier to be met as the plane lands. Never see them in their homes. Merely heading for the phone. Anonymous voices repeating the message, 'Jim and Carol Newmark, come to the White Courtesy desk to see your dad.' Yeah, Noah Newmark, the White Courtesy Phone father.

"Tell me, Dr. Feingold, what's life about? It's about work, right? Work and life are interchangeable. That's not healthy, you say? Well, who really cares?"

His reply catches him by surprise. He glances down at his uniform and blinks as he reviews his options. He'll have to find a phone booth and call Terry the Trickster. Breath-mint Terry T. and the camera-ready helper girls are waiting for him at a Styrofoam-covered drawbridge in the Hilltop Mall.

What can he say? "Go find yourself another bag man."

He turns off at the approach to West Valley College and Monte Sereno. He heads south for Highway 1 and Monterey. An hour later, he enters Santa Cruz, fabled city of the California Dream and vacation spot for migrating monarch butterflies, movie actor Rory (*How To Marry A Millionaire*) Calhoun's native town and the place where, in 1885, Cupid Kawananakoa, an Hawaiian prince walked out to sea with a board—thus introducing the sport of surfing to North America.

At last Noah pulls up at an aluminum and glass phone booth on Ocean Street near Denny's and, wiping a mixture of ash and sweat from his face, calls Terry the Trickster.

Next he calls the Doctor of Love in Monterey. "Long distance. It's an emergency, it's a damn emergency!" he hollers into the phone. "I'm calling from Los Angeles," he lies. "I'm Dr. Feingold's agent."

"Dr. Feingold's just leaving now," says the station manager. "She's heading back to her workshop."

"Good. Stop her before she goes out the door. Tell her to pick up the phone."

"Who the hell is this?" says Dr. F.

"Long distance, Dr. Feingold. My name is Noah Newmark, and I'm a Rent-A-Santa."

"Rent-A-Santa? Is this some kind of joke? Hmm. Noah Newmark. You're a journalist, aren't you?"

"Listen, you're a psychic. Don't you know every word I'm saying is true?"

"All right then, Newmark. What can I do for you?"

"My life has come unglued. I need to see you this afternoon."

"I'll be at the Mission Tile Motel in Monterey. Terra Cotta Seminar Room One. But remember, there are going to be other people there. I'll try to fit you in."

3

How to Succeed as St. Nick

Highway 1 to La Selva Beach. Watsonville. Moss Landing.
Brussels sprouts. Artichokes. Fort Ord. Sand City. Monterey.

On the drive down to Monterey, Noah recalls the job inter-view. How, earlier that month, at the commune, he joked with Holly about the Rent-A-Santa ad in the *Santa Cruz Cou-rier.* How, at last, he saw it as an opportunity.

"It's a great idea," Holly said, preparing breakfast. "Run it by your agent. You can do an inside Santa piece and a feature on Dr. Rama Pajama."

"Rama Pajama? Wait a minute, Holly. His name is Dr. Rama P. Rama."

"Rama Rama. Swami Salami. Salami Salami. What differ-ence does it make, Noah? Look at all the time you're spending on that *Champion of Living* story. Arranging appointments. Do-ing interviews. Taking photographs. Getting permissions. And there's no guarantee anyone will even run it. Get real. You're doing it on spec."

Noah looks up from the coffee he's brewing.

"Holly, that's not true, and you know it. We're here because I'm on assignment. *Our Times Magazine* is paying our expenses. Who knows? Later I may turn the *Champion* piece into a book."

Holly burns the toast.

"Oh, shit! Paying your expenses is no guarantee they'll pub-lish it. You may not get much more than a kill fee. And it's not something *The New Yorker* or *Vanity Fair* will want. Let's face it.

The oldest man on earth? The Champion of Living? It's been done before. What did you make last year, $75,000?"

"You know what I made, and it wasn't $75,000."

Holly puts another piece of bread into the toaster.

"Right, Noah. But what would the syndicates say to a Jewish Rent-A-Santa story? You've worked for them before. If you bring it off, it'll be reprinted year after year. Listen, you always said how envious you were as a child, that Christmas seemed like other peoples' holiday. Lots of people feel like that. Why not write about what it feels like as a Jew to get into the holiday, to enjoy Christmas for once from the outside in? Go underground for a while. Hang out with some of the other Santas. See how many of the Kris Kringles of this world are circumcised. Hell, Jesus was circumcised, wasn't he? What was his Hebrew name?"

"Yeshua," Noah answers.

"That's right, Yeshua. Yeshua H. Christ. And how do we know Santa himself isn't Jewish? Anyway, Christmas is a time for schlock—magazines will publish anything. You won't have to put your usual 100 hours into making it perfect.

"Don't look at me like that. It's true I'm the money-maker, but I believe in you and I want you to succeed. Who knows? What was that movie Jean Shepherd did about a kid wanting a Red Ryder air rifle? You remember."

Holly slices half a banana into her yogurt.

"A Christmas Story."

"Yeah, that's it. And you've still got some connections in the industry. But people have short memories. I'm glad you're taking time off. You know, you were a more exciting person when you weren't teaching. Besides, you keep saying you miss the fucking rat race."

"Have you finished?" Noah asks.

Holly looks to see if he's bristling.

"Magazines are my passion. Like being with you. You know, after we leave here, I'd like to spend more time in L.A. with you and Joey."

Holly bites hard on her lower lip.

"Nooky isn't passion. *Suffering*, that's what passion means. I'm a Catholic, remember. You're not a sufferer, Professor. You're a coupler—coupling and uncoupling like a box car. You and your dick. You and your five box cars. *Passion* he calls it."

Holly puts down her coffee. "You have a passion to conjugal and to write, to play baseball with your locker room buddies, and to tell stories."

"To conjugal?" Noah laughs.

"To get married. You know what I mean."

Holly reaches for Noah's hand.

"Honey, you've missed not being able to write as much as you want to."

"I wanted everything, the security of teaching and the excitement of being out there as a writer."

"So you lost what got you the job in the first place. I admit I thought it was a good move."

"So did I, Holly...I'm going to write my way back doing the stuff I want to do. Right now I guess I feel like a has-been."

Holly smiles and blinks back tears. "Noah, we can both use a change."

Noah chokes on his coffee.

"Admit it, the mystery's gone out of our marriage. We're both at a turning point. You've had it with Silver Screen College, and I need something besides *My Many Children*, something different, something challenging. Musical comedy. Maybe the movies. I can't count on playing Penelope forever. Shit, they could kill her off tomorrow." She folds and unfolds *The Courier*. "It's one big obituary."

"Huh?"

"Papers. Look, I know what you're up against. You want to write features. But look at today's paper, death, death and more death. Death is the media's idea of news. Drive-by killings, dismemberment and, sometimes for novelty, a little character assassination. Thank God for *Soap Opera Weekly.*"

Pencil in hand, Holly opens the latest *SOW* to the crossword puzzle. Test your Soap Opera IQ. "This is a good one, Noah. *Soap Scramblers*, they're not easy. If you're stumped, there's a 900 number you can call for clues," she says, looking up. "Isn't that sweet? This is what I do on the set when I have a break."

"You know, I tell my students the old ratio was 80–20 —80% bad news, 20% good news. Now it's more like 90–10 and the bad news is more bloodcurdling than ever. And I happen to be part of the game. But this Mt. Chakra story's different. That's one reason we're here, isn't it?"

"Sure, sure, but what if Rama Pajama's a fake? I mean, he has to be, right?"

"We'll see. I have this funny feeling...I don't think he's after power or sex or...Anyway, about your career, honey..." he pauses. "You're going to moonlight on top of your day-time soap?"

"Well, I thought...I'd work up to it gradually," she says, glancing up from the crossword puzzle, forefinger on number thirty-one across, 'Revlon rival.' I'd aim for, you know, *An Evening With Holly Hollander.* With a monologue and some of those songs of mine. The ones you say you like."

"Too risky. I'm against it."

Holly rolls her eyes.

"You know, at this point in your life you'd probably be the perfect husband for what's-her-name, Wife #1—or #2. You still want to settle down, don't you? Or maybe you want me to settle down and keep house for you. But that's not what I want. Maybe you don't believe in me, but Schumacher does. He thinks it's worth a try."

"What's this crap about Schumacher? What do you mean Schumacher believes in you?"

"I'm just telling you what he said, Noah. Schuie is my agent."

"Schuie's a taker—he exploits people—you said so yourself."

"Well..."

"I don't know how he does it," Noah shrugs.

"Does what?" Holly asks.

"Think about it, Holly. The man could win an Emmy for self-love. How can someone so astonished at his own good looks actually do something for someone else?"

Opening the refrigerator, Noah pulls out a carton of milk and a couple of eggs.

"I'm not going to listen to you," she squealed, hands over her ears.

"How many men's eyes water when they look at themselves in the mirror?" he said, dropping butter into a frying pan.

"Honey, where's the salt and pepper?"

"Jesus Christ, Noah, you look at yourself in the mirror. What's wrong with that? Admit it, honey, you're jealous."

"Of that shrink-wrapped boy-toy? Tell me, is the director of change making some kind of move on you?"

"That's not fair. Schumacher has my best interests at heart. And he's not trying to hold me down..."

Holly turns and retrieves the newspaper. A moment later, crinkles forming around her eyes, she puts down her coffee.

"Hey, did you read this article on macho fish? It made me think about my first husband."

"Macho fish? I guess I missed it."

"Well, in Africa there are male fish that compete with other male fish. Ten percent of the males dominate the food supply and all the female fish of their species. The macho fish are brighter colored than the wimp fish, the male majority. Macho fish have orange stripes and red and blue fins. Wimp fish are the color of sand and they don't even have sex. It's not allowed."

"Not allowed?"

"Macho fish won't allow the wimps to fuck. But macho fish are the first to get eaten by bigger fish because they're more colorful, you see? Then, when a macho dies, the wimps fight it out among themselves."

"Holly, what's your point?"

"Listen to me. Two or three days later, the wimp that wins over the other wimps starts growing orange stripes and red and blue fins. Even his balls grow bigger. Fish have balls, did you know that? But wimps who win, their balls double in size. And their brains grow bigger too. Successful fish are like successful men: success improves their looks and their brains. Anyway, in just a couple of days the ex-wimp controls the food supply and is busy screwing everything in sight."

"Like your ex, like Shyster Ned the shark? Holly, I'm listening, but I don't want to be a shark. What are you trying to say?"

"You know my first husband went off and had affairs."

"Yeah. So what?"

"Shyster Ned wanted to feel like a conqueror. You know why I kept my mouth shut for so long? Because when the bastard had affairs he became sexier at home. My feminist friends thought I was crazy. But I thought: why ruin the very thing you want? Besides, I was having affairs of my own. So I didn't ask too many questions.

"You know, in some cultures women walk a couple steps behind the male to make him feel like a big shot. Okay, letting Ned sleep around was my way of walking a couple steps behind the jerk. It made him feel good and he performed better for it, as a lover and as a lawyer.

"It's in a woman's interest to build up her man so he looks and acts dominant. That's all. My feminist friends call me a throw-back. They can say what they like, but I know a woman is better off when her man is better looking, has bigger balls and bigger brains, than the next man. Even if it means being a shark."

"God, Holly, what did I do before I met you? In the old days people used to ask, 'Are you a man or a mouse?' But you say men are either small-balled, fish-brained wimps or sharks. Is that right?"

"I just want you to pick some hot topics for a change. Maybe you ought to do something on macho men. Or why so many women are still attracted to sharks despite thinking they want sensitive, nurturing types."

"Well, I don't like the sound of it. Any of it. What are you planning? I know you, fox lady. You're up to something."

"Ah, come on, let's dance and stop this nonsense."

Putting on a tape of Sade Adu's *Promise*, arms around the would-be Santa's neck, Holly slides one hand down his back. She keeps the other around his neck. Holds him tight. They go on dancing to the song *War of the Hearts*.

An hour later Noah brews up a pot of strong coffee while Holly goes back to browsing in the paper.

"Holly, I'm going to have to run. They stop interviewing at noon."

Holly looks up from the Entertainment section.

"Oh, wow, look at this. There's going to be a Father Christmas World Congress in Denmark with hundreds of Santa's attending from all over the world. Someone should fly over and cover the event."

"There's synchronicity for you. I have a feeling if we're not careful that newspaper is going to change our lives. Remember," Noah says kissing her goodbye, "no unilateral decisions. No surprises. We agreed to talk things over first, right?"

4

The Interview

Santa Cruz, California

A buxom aspiring female Santa Claus in her quilted down jacket swaggers out of room C-I in the Santa Cruz Civic Auditorium.

Noah Newmark is next in line for the Rent-A-Santa interview.

"Ho ho ho," she says over her shoulder, giving Noah an unnerving sidelong glance, a sort of knowing sneer ("I know what you're here for") tinged with Christmas spirit, Santa Claus one-upmanship. She's warring with him for the job of Santa Claus.

"Ho ho ho, yourself," Noah answers, wondering what he, at age 6, would have made of a big-breasted female Santa Claus.

"Are you Santa Claus," he might have asked.

"I'm Ms. Santa Claus. Mr. Santa Claus is home making dinner."

Apart from Joey, Noah's children are away with their mothers. "I want to be Santa because I know how much I'll be missing them," he plans to tell the personnel officer. "I want to be Santa so I can give love and gifts to other children. If I can't personally give these things to my own children, I can at least try to give them to other people's children."

Noah hasn't practiced his "Ho ho ho," but plans to wing it. "Ho ho ho" from the diaphragm, "ho ho ho" from the heart.

Noah wants to be Santa Claus.

His qualifications?

He has a beard. He's Jewish, and for 47 years he's fantasized about participating not as an envious outsider, but as a whole-hearted Christmas insider. What better way than to become the plump, white-bearded old man himself?

His shortcomings?

He is 6' 2" tall, broad shouldered and muscular, more circuit slugger than Santa. At 180 pounds, he has a lean, hungry look about him, sad hazel-brown eyes and a slightly hooked nose.

The door to room c-1 opens and the Santa Claus personnel officer—a brunette—invites Noah inside. "Ah, Mr. Newmark," she beams. She has a cheery, British accent and, Mary Poppins like, introduces him to her assistant, Allen. "I say, don't you think Mr. Newmark has a splendid beard?" The two interviewers sit at one end of a mahogany conference table and Noah sits at the other.

"Mr. Newmark, to start off would you give us a sample of your 'Ho ho ho?'"

Noah stands, takes a deep breath and, summoning up all the jolliness he can muster, roars, "Ho ho ho."

The two personnel officers nod approvingly and make notes on their lined yellow pads. Noah is feeling more at ease.

"What are the names of Santa's reindeer?"

"Comet. Dancer. Prancer. Blitzen...Rudolph...hmm."

Noah gets only four out of eight right. He's failing. What the hell is he doing here? A 47-year-old ex-sports writer trying to get a job as Santa Claus and failing.

"I don't even know the names of my eight stinking reindeer."

"There's Dancer, Prancer, Comet, Vixen, Cupid, Donner, Blitzen..." they correct Santa. "And Rudolph doesn't really count. He's a latecomer."

Next question.

"What would you say if you had a kid sitting in your lap and he pulled off your beard?" asks the assistant Santa Claus personnel officer.

"Well, I'd say something like, 'See, I have a real beard, but it's red because I'm young. And I wear an all-white fake beard so I'll look older than I really am. People expect Santa to have an all-white beard. But now you know the truth. I'm younger than people think.'"

What a ridiculous answer, Noah thinks.

To his surprise, the two interrogators nod approvingly. Again, they write something on their pads.

"Why do you want to be Santa Claus?" they ask.

Noah is ready for them. They're wondering if I'm a child molester or a drug addict. He controls himself. They're only doing their job. They don't want a Santa Claus who's going to arrive at some Christmas office party too ripped to climb out of his sleigh. Noah tells the interviewers about his children and how much he misses them.

"What will you say if children ask how come they didn't get what they wanted last Christmas?"

"I'd say Santa Claus loves them and tries to give children what he thinks they most need. That he has many children to give things to—children in all parts of the world—and that some years he runs out of presents before he's finished. But that he tries to make up for it the next year."

"Okay, but remember Santa Claus never makes promises," mumbles the assistant. "Also you may be asked to appear in some unusual ways."

Noah imagines the scene: a Rent-A-Stripper with a long white beard and a bag of toys jumping naked out of a cake.

The recruiter explains: "Last year our Santa was met at the end of a deserted mountain road with a horse-drawn wagon filled with hay. You want to be prepared for anything."

"And Santa does not use drugs and he does not accept drinks," says Ms. Poppins. "No liquor. No drugs."

"What if he's invited to stay for dinner?"

"Santa Claus does not accept dinner invitations."

The interview ends with the personnel officers asking Noah to make up a story. Noah's imagination fails him. He can think of nothing to say. He's written features, columns and news stories. But now he sits at the mahogany conference table with nothing to say. "I bombed," says Noah under his breath. "I need a drink, I think."

"What's that, Mr. Newmark?" says Mary drawing herself up to her full height. Ms. Poppins has shiny dark hair and small peering blue eyes.

"Oh, nothing. I'm thirsty," he mumbles.

"Thank you, then. We'll call Thursday or Friday of next week."

Thursday and Friday pass with no word.

The following Tuesday Ms. Poppins calls.

"Noah Newmark?" says the voice at the other end of the line, "Congratulations. You're Santa Claus."

Noah immediately begins wondering if there hasn't been some mistake. "Me? Santa? Surely there must be a hundred aspiring Santas out there better qualified than me. Over-sized actors with droll little mouths and long white beards. Accomplished, 300-pound dimple-faced singers of Christmas carols. Red-nosed, pot-bellied reindeer ranchers."

The truth is, Noah is scared. Having gotten the job, he doesn't know if he's up to it. "I know it's a lark, but think of the responsibility," he says to Holly. "*Sinter Klaas*...a supernatural being who brings happiness and who is supposed to know the names, addresses and dreams of every child on earth. Who knows the good ones from the bad and who loves both equally? Who has unconditional love for everyone, even noisy, runny-nosed, sneezy children who whine and cry and pull his beard. Is that me? David Newmark's son?"

And what if he forgets or calls his reindeer by the wrong names? Cutie, Blitzen, Bagel and Vixen. Donder, Dasher, Schwartzkopf and Prancer, like some New York law firm?

The journalist buys a copy of Clement C. Moore's *The Night Before Christmas,* a facsimile of the original 1848 edition, and writes down reindeer names in his Day-Timer for reference and study. Planning his new feature, he goes to the library and reads everything he can on Christmas. Putting aside his appointment book, he opens a set of 3 x 5 index cards and writes:

- Clement C. Moore was a scholar of Hebrew and a poet. The father of nine children, he wrote *The Night Before Christmas* to be read on Christmas Eve in the privacy of his own home to his children. He was greatly annoyed when a friend picked up a copy of the poem and published it, without his consent, in *The Troy Sentinel*, December 23, 1823.

- The historical Saint Nicholas, born in the third century, became bishop of Myra in Asia Minor and was famous for giving gifts and presents during the time of the winter solstice. Saint Nicholas is also known as the patron saint and guardian of children, students, virgins and sailors.

- In Holland, Saint Nicholas appeared for centuries as a medieval bishop—red miter on his head, long ecclesiastical *cope* draped from his shoulders. In America, the red miter and long *cope* became the bright red cap and suit of Santa Claus.

- In Austria, Santa Claus is accompanied by a female bogey, a hag called Buzebergt, who carries a pot of starch to smear on peoples' faces and a rod to beat naughty children.

- Number of letters that must be moved to change Santa into Satan: 1
- Price paid at auction for a 1942 Christmas card signed by Adolf Hitler: $3,025.

Mt. Chakra

To his surprise, Holly is not only supportive, but seductive. She begins by opening a bottle of Cabernet Sauvignon, and snuggling close. "I'll be your make-up artist. Later, you'll try on that suit and beard. You're going to play Santa but you'll see. You'll become Father Christmas himself. Don't I become the parts I play?

"Give me my fantasy, Noah," she says, unbuttoning her blouse.

Arching her back, she invites Noah to undo her bra. She slips off her walking shoes, wiggles her toes.

"We'll practice in bed so you'll really understand from the inside. Did you ever hear of the casting couch? It's a variation on the Stanislavsky method. First you get into the part, and then you make out just as the character you're playing would make out. It's not as easy as it sounds."

"Well, I wouldn't want to go through something like that with someone who hadn't had the experience. Will you be my acting coach?"

"I'll play acting coach and director-seductress. If you please me, I'll help with costume and make-up. And remember, it'll add something to your story. Now, put away your notebook and take off your clothes or I'm going to audition someone else."

"I don't know. It doesn't feel right," Noah says, throwing back the wine.

"Getting undressed? Slipping into bed with the director? Noah, I'm offended. You know, you have to appeal to your lover's imagination. Everyone knows that."

"Come on," Noah laughs. "You miss the point. I'm thinking about playing Santa. I'm uptight about that. What will my father think? He's a professional comic, remember? He'll do a number on me. He'll slaughter me."

Sighing, Holly gets back into the moment.

"He's a tough old dude, but I like your dad."

"Hmm. Of all my wives, I think he likes you the best. You're like a daughter to him."

Holly cuts up an apple and plunges a slice into her mouth.

"He approves of me because I'm making money."

"My father approves of anyone who makes money. The more money they make, the more he approves of them. And he likes it that you can account for every penny you make."

"He approves of me more than he approves of you?" she says, reaching for a hairbrush.

"Knowing my Dad, he probably does. I'm like that fifty-dollar bill in his joke about the rabbi."

"Tell me."

"It's the Sabbath and a rabbi is walking out of his synagogue when a fifty-dollar bill falls out of his pocket. One of his students sees it and is horrified. 'Sir, how can you violate the commandment against carrying money on *Shabbas?*'"

"The rabbi bends to pick up the fifty-dollar bill, 'Oh, this? You call this money?'"

"In his mind, I'm not making enough money to be taken seriously. What a writer makes—what a teacher makes—is small change. You're making money. You he takes seriously."

"Then where does love come into it?"

"You've heard him. 'Love is a fine thing, but love with noodles is even tastier.' He's a comedian. He isn't against romance. He's just *pro* noodles."

"Pro noodles? That's a new one. I know he's pro whiskey.

But I haven't heard of anyone being pro noodles."

Holly pours more wine and, crossing her legs, sits up in bed.

"When we were in Chicago last year, your father had to bait me. So he told me the first thing an Orthodox Jewish man does when he wakes up in the morning is to say, 'Thank God I'm not a woman.' What do you think of that? The old geezer knew I'd be pissed. I confess, I didn't let him off too easy."

"Holly, he was just trying to get a rise out of you."

"Well, he got his *rise*. What annoys me is I'm almost as bad as he is. That's pretty funny, isn't it? I thank God for some of the things I'm not, too."

"What do you thank God for?" Noah says.

"Say I'm in an elevator and I see a woman five feet tall. I think, 'Thank God I'm not short.' Meanwhile, she's thinking, 'That looks like that heavy woman on TV. What's her name? Penelope? It can't be. Must be Penelope's not-so-glamorous understudy.'"

"Holly, you're amazing. You're gorgeous. But tell me, is there any woman who doesn't torment herself thinking she's too fat, or too thin, or too short, or too tall, or too something?

"Each of my wives has been critical of her good looks. That's five women in a row. Maybe it's me. I'm beginning to feel guilty. Maybe it's something I'm doing."

"Guilt?" says Holly. "Feel guilt about being drawn to the little baby in women that women are trying to escape from. Feel guilt about playing the patriarch who tries to keep them that way. Feel guilt about walking out on the women who do the most for you. Feel guilt about any damn thing you feel like."

"Holly," he says at six the next morning in bed, the fragrance of her still in his beard, her blonde hairs intermingled with his red ones, "do I seem, you know, somehow different?"

"What do you mean, Noah?" Holly rolls over on her side.

Noah can feel waves of warmth moving between her belly and his.

"It's crazy," he murmurs.

"What's crazy?"

"That it's possible to feel the foreplay to heartache, the foreplay to heartsick. I feel like I'm coming down with heartsore," he says as he might say, "I'm coming down with the flu."

"I don't understand. What is this, more gamesmanship?"

"Holly, I've been dreaming, that's all. Something that puzzled me is suddenly clear. That just as in sex there's foreplay, the act itself, and afterplay, there are three stages to the breakup of a relationship."

"I don't want to hear it. You're a heavy dude, and you're not making sense."

"It has nothing to do with us. I'm just thinking, that's all. Tell me what you think. To my mind, first there's the preliminary, the preliminary to a breakup stage. Then there's the breakup itself. And, finally, the heartsick, heartsore, heartbreak that follows. That's the afterplay stage. But in any one stage of lovemaking, or love-leaving, all the others are already there. They're there like seeds of some kind. You know what I mean, Holly?"

"All I know is that when it comes to breakup, you're a connoisseur. You're one of those people who live for subtleties. You know, there are breakup connoisseurs just as there are wine connoisseurs. I have an idea. Why don't you try reducing your vocabulary by thirty words a day? Who knows, it could improve our communication. Don't sulk, Noah. Tell me what you're thinking."

"That word you just used, *subtleties*. It's made up of two words. *Subtle ties*. After a breakup, it is precisely those subtle ties one's heart longs to have restored."

Holly reaches for a nail file.

"I give up."

Noah turns, fumbles for some matches, lights a couple sticks of sandalwood incense and silently prays.

O God, reduce my vocabulary by thirty words a day. And while you're at it, Lord, I know many people require discipline to work. I need discipline not to work. Or so she says. 'Noah, put some effort into relaxing.' Working is relaxing. Not working causes stress. That's what it's like for me. But I'm working on it. Please, Lord, all I ask is to lighten up.

O God, bring her back.

"I was dreaming of you," he says.

In the dream, Holly, sweet Holly, had left him to go off to a party and he watched as she flirted with a thirty-something man. Trying to make himself heard, Noah called across the room. He knew his wife heard him calling, and he knew she had her attention fixed on the thirty-something stranger and was, for that reason, refusing to answer. So next he called as he had never before called to her. He called with a voice that was soundless, a voice that was no voice at all.

Even in the dream Noah realized his wife knew if he reproached her saying, for instance, "Holly, I just called to you. Didn't you hear me?" she'd respond, "What am I, a psychic? How can you expect me to have heard you?" And she'd be right. Of course she was coming on to the guy, more than flirting, but had she betrayed him? And though he knew in the dream she'd been with other men, not just Jack Thirty-something, he knew he couldn't do anything about it. He knew in the dream, even as he dreamed he knew what was going on, that he was going to refuse to accept that anything out of the ordinary had happened.

Because, at that point, there was no physical evidence to suggest that anything had. And he felt certain he could win her back. And it would be easier to win her back if he didn't admit to himself, or to her, that he knew just how close their marriage was to being over.

"Goddamnit, it's over." The words well up in him like a mantra. "It's over." Noah clamps his jaw shut to keep from saying them in her face. "It's over. It's over."

Burrowing under his pillow, he murmurs sleepily, "Block that intuition. Suppress that thought."

"Hey, Noah, don't go back to sleep. You asked me something. Do you seem different? How do you mean *different?*"

"Holly, when I talk to myself, in my mind, I mean, I address myself as Santa. I try not to let it bother me. But it's sometimes strange, really strange. I mean, don't you think so?"

Holly yawns and stretches.

"Not at all," she laughs. "It's like I said before. You're just getting used to the part. Trust me, Noah. You'll make a great Santa—and you'll write a syndicated piece about it."

8:00 A.M.

Noah ambles into the kitchen to brew some coffee. He comes back with fresh-squeezed orange juice, hot buttered bagels, cream cheese and jam. And a rose, lifted the day before from the community greenhouse.

"Madame, breakfast is served."

Placing the tray on Holly's knees, he bows. Then joins her in bed.

What can he do to make her laugh? No matter what obstacles there may be in a relationship, if you can make your partner laugh, that person will stay with you. Noah feels a sudden need to make her laugh.

"You know that Tommy Dorsey tune:
  Sitting in my lala
  waiting for my yaya, Noah sings.

"Anyway, I taught it to Joey. Then the other night, while you were away, I took him to the movies—that Jerry Lewis film, *The Nutty Professor.* I bought him a Hershey bar. Just as the film started he said this amazing thing: 'I'm watching candy with my eyes. I'm eating candy with my mouth. Dad, this is living.'"

Holly laughs and shakes her head. "The kid takes after me," she says, sipping orange juice.

Hesitating for a moment, Noah puts his lips to her eyelids, then lightly massages her shoulders.

"Holly, sweetheart, is it true that romantics make love with their eyes shut and realists make love with their eyes open?"

"Where did you hear that?" she asks.

"I read it in *Kama Sutra.*"

Holly snorts.

"What difference does it make if one's eyes are open or shut?" Holly wants to know.

"Romantics do it with their eyes shut because it helps them concentrate on an ideal, a vision of some sort in their heads.

"It's the realists who keep their eyes open and go all out for atmosphere: flowers, candles, soft music, incense."

"Noah, you're crazy," she laughs. "You know that?"

Yes. Thank God. He has actually been able to make her laugh. Question two: what can he do to keep romance alive? Noah has read everything he can on the subject.

"Create surprises," one author suggested. "Take her to the opera. Write poems for her. Take her shopping. Buy sexy clothes for her. Pamper her as she approaches forty or fifty. Those end-of-the-decade birthdays are hell for marriages."

He sings, playing the part of a sappy young lover.

...Pink light round your white body,
   your blue eyes flashing,

"You've been around the track a few times. I'm not your first date," Holly laughs. "Speaking of tracks, if you were a horse, you'd be a long shot."

"What are you talking about?"

"A four-time loser. A bad bet. Oh, Noah, don't frown. I'm only joking."

Her eyes widen. She takes a last sip of coffee, pushes away the tray and reaches over to caress him. Again, she guides Santa, pressing lightly on his shoulders. Soon he tastes her still moist from the night before. At the same time she presses his hands to her large, soap-smooth breasts.

"Oh God," she moans, "I want it, I want..." Santa pulls off his red nightshirt as Holly rolls over on her belly and comes up on all fours. Hazel eyes closed, he kisses and strokes her fragrant valentine. "I'm Dancer, I'm Prancer. I'm Comet," she hollers.

Santa pulls her to him. Holly climbs on top. Mr. and Mrs. Claus kiss.

She rolls away from him. He prays.

Dear wife. Don't leave. Don't leave.

5

Mirror, Mirror

Mt. Chakra

Noah reels out of the bathroom and watches as Holly, at her dressing table, lips moving, brushes her hair. She's about to begin her ritual singing of verses, song lyrics to build her confidence.

> *Mirror, mirror, on the wall,*
> *who is the fairest of them all?*

Assuming the role of a singing ventriloquist, Holly answers her own question. But this time there's an edge to her singing. She goes beyond self-compliment.

Her mirror replies:

> *You are, Holly darling, and your life is a ball.*
> *You're rich, you're famous*
> *but your husband spoils...all.*

Noah overhears the soft singing and knows what he's hearing is burlesque, but he can't make out all the words.

"What did you say? That husband of yours *what?*"

"Oh, Noah, it's just a song."

Song or not, he can't help wincing each time her voice breaks, a signal to him she's under pressure, a signal something—someone?—is waiting in the wings. He bites his lip.

For her part, Holly is pleased with the mirror's report. She opens a bottle of Perrier and takes a sip.

Turning on the fan, she hums thoughtfully for a moment, and then sings:

First I wake,
and then I shower.
This is...finest hour.
I put the glass to my lips
take two...refreshing sips.
The day is bright
my heart is light.
The camera loves me
day and night.

"Mmm, darling, you're terrific," she burbles and gives herself a hug.

She's having trouble pumping herself up. After ten years of marriage, he knows the more *moon-June* verses she sings, the more nervous she is. This is a ritual, he reminds himself. This is Actress Magic. This is something Holly does each day out of habit. Is he lying to himself? Is it possible that her morning ritual is a way for her to avoid talking to him?

His face darkens. Will they be together a year from now? What if he doesn't fit into her plans anymore? All this good sex may itself be a sign the marriage is over. It's happened before to Noah. The great lovemaking that precedes a breakup, the let-it-go-on-forever-honey fucking that comes out of the sometimes desperate, don't-leave-me-or-I'll die, strenuous and all-out effort to re-assert one's authority. *Yentzer* sex, Shelley, his first wife, called it, "sexual athleticism."

Marriage #1 was ending and, typically, ambivalent, feeling guilty, trying to reawaken the spark, or at least giving it a chance, knowing all the while he would be leaving, he was doing what he could to save it. Suspecting his motives, Shelley Levine would tease him, call him Mr. Yentzer. "There you go, Mr. Yentzer, warming up for the Olympics." She knew one-for-the-road sex when she saw it. "Sex with a smile," she called it. "Yentzer sex is good sex, honey, but it's like sex with a smile: 'Sex to speed the parting guest.'" And she was right. Life #1. Wife #1, he sometimes called her. What if Holly knew, what if he told her, he dreamed sometimes of getting back together with Wife #1?

Will it work now? This time he really wants to save the marriage. But he knows the odds are against him. To look at her, you might think they'd spent the night watching *I Love Lucy* re-runs. What if it were too late? What if it turned out that their parts were reversed? What if it turned out Holly was calling the shots and playing Yentzer, the traditionally male role?

"Holly," he says, massaging her neck, "I have the sense all is not well in the boudoir."

Holly fumbles in her makeup drawer, but says nothing.

He goes to the closet to find his slippers.

Turning up the fan to High, applying mascara, Holly sings:

Life is...
fame is fleeting.
Seize the day. It's...or never.
So...for it, Ms. Hollander.
Better indiscreet
...obsolete.
Yes, elite you are. Petite you're not.
You've got a...who forgives a lot.

Searching in the closet, he has trouble making out exactly what it is she's saying. All he knows is that when she's feeling anxious, she says things she doesn't mean. At such times she means only half the things she says. The more biting she is, the more vulnerable she's feeling.

Then again, she could just be rehearsing, trying out lines, scenes, songs—attitudes—for the next episode of *My Many Children*.

Besides, she's acting right in character with the part she plays. It's not Holly. It's gruff, soap show Penelope at the dressing table.

Penelope with her husky, up-all-night rasp voice. Penelope of whom Charlie Schumacher said, "She's daytime's hottest hedonist. She has a license to be perverse."

Schumacher. Noah clenches and unclenches his fists. Schumacher with his goatskin loafers. Square-jaw Schumacher with his silver cigarette case. Schumacher and his fucking press releases: "buxom blonde barracuda scavenging for sex and trouble, Holly Hollander *is* blue-eyed, gap-toothed Penelope, the Queen of Mean...see her evil-doing pizzazz in today's episode...titillating, watchable high trash...a made-for-TV vixen villainess..."

"Charlie, do you ever think about the swill you're putting out to *Soap Opera Days* and the rest of those magazines?" Noah once complained. "Our lives are not exactly pay-for-view television. I've got four children who have to deal with this stuff."

"Calm down, Newmark. What are you on about?" said the agent of change.

"Your wife lives on Planet Hollywood. A limo comes every morning to take her to work. She's famous, do you understand? Gimme a break."

"I'll give you a break alright," Noah said, and had had to be restrained from punching Schumacher.

Noah had grown up believing that if the sex was good, then all else in a relationship was good. That he understood to be one of the great truths of marriage.

Forgetting his slippers, Noah returns and kisses the back of Holly's neck.

"What did you say in that song of yours...*forgives a lot?* or something?"

"Noah, you're not taking my rhymes seriously..."

He bites her ears. He picks up, juggles and catches the silver-handled hairbrush. Begins brushing her hair. Presses a few damp strands up and off the back of her head. He reaches inside her slip and runs his hand along her spine.

Noah speaks to the reflected image of his wife.

"Sometimes, sweetheart, I wonder if I can ever come close to loving you as much as you love yourself. I'm your biggest fan, but sometimes I feel you lumping me in with your public."

There's more to the morning ritual than applying make-up. Holly is ready now to sharpen her wits. He's the sparring partner. Noah enjoys the verbal jabbing, the punching and counter punching. And they don't need a script or someone to write material to engage in their sparring matches. All they need is to raid their everyday life.

Holly stamps her slippered foot, pulls back from the dressing table, and dances wildly about the room.

His heart racing, Noah steadies himself by saying his mantra.

> Holly is larger than life. Holly is a prime example
> of what women are. Other women are like this
> to a lesser or greater degree, but she's divinely,
> perversely, excruciatingly excessive.

He took a certain pride in aligning himself with what he regarded as an archetype. Danger, O danger!

"Didn't you dance about like that on television?" he laughs. "Yeah, I remember now. I saw it on *My Many Children*. Your mindless producer's idea of a bacchanalia."

"Hey, I'm only a soap opera actress, but you and your five wives, *five wives*! That's not a bacchanalia?" Holly shakes her head. "Don't talk about me. I'm not going to let you put me down because of the work I do."

"Who's putting you down? I'm proud of you. You're the one who's having doubts about your career."

Holly seems not to hear this. Half Penelope and half herself, she's off and running.

"You've scripted your life. Talk about soap opera. Talk about bacchanalia. And who am I to your friends? The fifth Mrs. Newmark. Act Five, Scene Five, Holly Hollander, an appendage to her husband's domestic comedy.

"Sometimes I feel we're just a couple kids playing house. Do you ever have that feeling? That we're only pretending to live together."

"What's wrong with being kids? Kids get to have fun," Noah says.

"Maybe that's the problem. Maybe that's it. Your idea of fun is looking words up in dictionaries. Being married to you is like being married to Mr. Thesaurus. You're a Pie-in-the-Sky scribbler, you and your Big Rock-Candy Mountain guru. This isn't the 1960s, and if it's enlightenment you're looking for, I'll give you enlightenment. This place is boring. Mt. Chakra, they call it. Better re-name it Mt. Tofu. I'm bored, Noah. I'm bored with you. Bored, bored, bored."

Noah sneaks a look at himself in the mirror. Maybe he is boring. Even Holly's cohorts, as they call themselves, regard him as a dry-humored journalist, a man incapable of writing puff pieces, definitely not a fun guy.

"Actually, you know, Rama's not boring," says Holly. "He's the most interesting man around this place. He's his own person. And the dude has a pretty good sense of humor for someone who lives in a cave and doesn't get laid."

"You think having sex and having a sense of humor are the same thing?"

"Of course they are. As my character Penelope says, 'You can't have good sex without humor, and you can't have good humor without sex.'"

Noah laughs.

"You know something else I like about Rama Pajama?" Holly goes on, "I like what he says about money."

"Money?"

"Yes, money. He's more worldly than you think, Noah. He says, THE ANSWER IS MONEY. WHAT IS THE QUESTION? EVERYTHING.

"Now that's what I call enlightenment."

6

The Note

Santa Cruz

Boxes of Christmas treats on the back seat, Holly's gold bracelet, Joey's baseball cards and Legos in hand, he bursts into the guest house. "Hey, guys, I'm home!" Crouching to keep from hitting his head, he steps into the bedroom with the gold shag, wall-to-wall carpet. There is a note lying on the pillow.

> *Noah, sorry to leave you like this. No use talking. Please understand…this is…my big chance. Taking Joey. It's now or never. Flying out tonight…N.Y.C…Jo Beth Winter's. It's going to be alright, need time. Don't come after me.*

"It's going to be all right? It's going to be all right for the marriage? For eight-year-old Joey?" he sobs. "Who the fuck is this going to be all right for? It's going to be all right for her, or at least that's what she's hoping. She's leaving. She's scared and is leaving a note for me not intended for me at all, but to reassure herself.

"Joey, is that you?" he says, hearing the door slam. Noah turns, expecting to see Joey come racing into the room. Joey. Joey who had given him the idea for this new story. Joey who, having heard from his teacher that there was a 101-year-old doctor 'alive and kicking' in the Santa Cruz Mountains, had run home flushed with excitement. "He's the oldest man on earth. Dad, dad, take us to see the Champion of Living."

"The Champion of Living." Noah had said. "Good for

you, son! Yeah, okay, we'll check him out. But you know, Joey, there are people even older than that."

He steps into the kitchen, reaches into the refrigerator and uncaps a beer.

"Oh, God." Hands shaking, he sets down the beer, forces his hands into his pockets and clenches his fists. The hands spring out again. He tries holding them under his shirt, pressing his fingers into his armpits. All at once both hands vault into the room. They're everywhere. Massaging the back of his neck. Cupping his Adam's apple. Stroking his forehead. They reach at last for some crumpled papers on the kitchen table. He watches as his hands unfold the scented note.

…Flying out tonight … This is my big chance…

Noah reaches for his old mitt—the one he travels with, never leaves behind. This is the last game of a crucial series. He's pitching for Chicago against the Yankees. It's the top of the ninth, and neither team has scored. He's got wives at first, second and third. In fact, he's got two wives at third. Holly steps up to the plate ready to knock his next pitch over the centerfield bleachers. Does he have what it takes to get the ball past her? Noah knows he can do it. But here comes his manager strolling out to the mound.

"I'm gonna give that new guy, that left-hander, Schumacher, a shot at her," says the manager.

"Goddamn you," Noah protests.

"That's it, Newmark, you're off the team."

7

The Two-Hearted Healer

God will provide—if only God
would provide until God provides.
—Jewish saying

Mission Tile Motel, Monterey - Terra Cotta Seminar Room One

Felicia Feingold, the Doctor of Love, is a loose-limbed, 35-year-old brunette storyteller. Celebrant and hostess, she flashes a come-on-let's-lighten-up-and-have-some-fun smile. She wears silver and turquoise bracelets and rings, a bear claw necklace and black stretch pants and a black sweater. She resembles Elizabeth Taylor, if you can imagine Elizabeth Taylor in her prime with a stethoscope, laughing at her own jokes and lecturing on How to Heal a Broken Heart, waving a ceremonial knife and summoning up energy from her feet and healing people.

As Noah enters pink Terra Cotta Seminar Room One and adjusts his jacket, he is welcomed with hoots of laughter. "Why it's Father Christmas," says a workshop groupie wearing a white-on-black tribal print jumpsuit. "It's the Christmas Patriarch," exclaims another, looking up from her Day-Timer, "what the hell is he doing here?"

Waterglass in hand, Dr. Feingold turns toward Noah and winks seductively. "This is my special guest, journalist Noah Newmark," she says, raising the glass as if in salute. *"Shalom,* Santa. Umm, we have some private business to discuss after the workshop, don't we? Seriously though, Santa is a sensitive fellow. He's asked to interview me before he lifts off with his sleigh.

"So, how about it? Let's show him some holiday spirit."

Dubiously, the workshop communicants—women ages 30 to 60—applaud.

"Wait a minute. There's been a mistake," Noah says, heading for an exit.

"Please wait, my friend. We're only joking. You're welcome here and we'd like you to stay. That's right. There are some empty seats toward the back."

A wave of grief sweeps over him. What would Jay Grimm, his old pitching coach, say? "Hang in there and tough it out, Newmark." "Okay, I'll hear her out," he decides, his heart racing.

"The truth comes concealed in all sorts of packages," Dr. Feingold reminds her audience. "More likely than not, it'll come without ribbons. Or were you expecting this pearl, this jewel, to come in the form of a man? Well, rest easy. It's not the men in your lives. You're far more likely to find that gem in yourself than in some man. You're it, my friends. *You* are the package..."

Dr. Feingold appears to have the power to generate energy as she needs it. Noah watches as she cranks up the charisma. He can see she's reaching her climax, her peroration to a three-day workshop. He turns on his tape recorder *and* prepares to take notes. Each time he does a story, the words he hears and writes—the written account—subtly differs from what he manages to pick up with his tape recorder. Sometimes he writes whole sentences that he hears, sentences that his sources confirm, but that the tape machine misses. Other times the tape recorder picks up details the writer misses. In order to get it all, every sentence, every inflection, every word, and to provide double the evidence in case he's sued, Noah simultaneously writes and tapes what people say.

"Your heart is your only child," says Dr. Feingold to her audience. "And when the spiritual heart opens, your womb opens, too. Fill your wombs with light, friends. The womb as a prune is no place for life."

Writing those sentences, Noah puts check marks by the words *womb* and *prune*. One day he'll do a story on Dr. Feingold and this upside-down mission tile *shul*...

He scribbles:

> Upside-down *shul*? In an orthodox synagogue, the men sit together in rows up front, and the women, prohibited from singing prayers, sit in the back behind a curtain. With Felicia Feingold, the women lead the action, women are the congregation, and the men sit in the back behind a velvet belt.

Over the years Noah has developed a system of symbols and squiggles. These barely legible markings enable him to write as fast as Dr. Feingold speaks.

"Tell me, friends, wouldn't a little cushion of energy make your life more pleasant?" Felicia goes on. "And letting go of guilt can increase your cushion of energy.

"You know what empowerment means? It means letting go of your guilt."

Her voice is raspy, ironic, teasing.

Smiling, the women nod.

"Mary. Mary was a priestess, by the way. Mary, you know, ran the Church for thirty years after Jesus' death. That's a fact."

Noah lingers in the back of the conference room wiping perspiration from his forehead. Should he hang around or leave? He feels outnumbered, one of only two men in the midst of a devoted, shiny-faced sisterhood.

Letting the suspense build, pausing for a moment, Dr. Feingold sits on the massage table—center stage—and swings her fine legs. To the right of the table is an American flag, a smaller golden bear California flag and, to the left, a Christmas tree.

Noah sketches Dr. Feingold. He draws arrows pointing to

Dr. Feingold's face. Beside one he writes, *porcelain-capped teeth.* Beside another, *Elizabeth Taylor facial mole,* and, in double quotes, he jots, "*reconnecting to the Kundalini Energy.*"

The room smells of pine needles, coffee and mulled wine. Chocolates, orange blossom aerosol, green olives, mayonnaise, sour dough, pumpernickel and brie. Hors d'oeuvres and a smorgasbord of perfumes. Even as Felicia Feingold speaks, a few hungry women approach the linen-covered table.

Noah finds a seat in the back row next to a white-bearded man of about sixty wearing work boots and a plaid shirt.

"Hello, Santa. Welcome to the Groovy People Seminar," says the man, extending a thickly callused hand missing one finger. "Hey, ol' Buddy, what are you doing here?"

"As you heard, I've got an appointment with the love doctor," Noah laughs. "What about you?"

"Keep an eye on my missus. Larry's the name," he says, extending his hand. "I'm a rancher."

"I'm Noah Newmark," says Noah, in the middle of the handshake.

"Yeah. I know your work. You're an old sports reporter, aren't you? I read your stuff in *The Gazette.* You lost your missus? Mine's all ready to go. She's got her suitcases packed. They're in the trunk of our damn Chevy."

"So why's she here?" asks Noah.

"Women get together and they become witchy. Can't you smell it, buddy? Essence of Lady Upstarts. That's what I call it. And Feingold is a made-for-TV general..."

"A general?"

"It's war against men," says Larry. "Don't be taken in. They're disciplined and tough. All those hours they spend working out! I'm telling you, Feingold's not what she seems."

"Well," says Noah. "I like the look of her. A show-biz

entertainer who's good at what she does. Maybe an authentic healer. I mean, why not?"

"You're a newspaperman. You should know better," says the rancher, turning away. "Well, at least she's not coming on like some New Age hooker, one of those gals claiming to be a mouthpiece for the ascended masters."

Catching the attention of a dyed, blonde-haired woman in the front row, Dr. Feingold takes a deep breath.

"If there's trouble in your marriage," she says, "and you know it's over, forget it. If it's really gone bad, no amount of trying is going to fix it."

"Kk-Karen!" cries Larry, rising to his feet. The blonde ignores him.

"Did you see that?" Larry groans. "She won't even look at me now."

"As we learned in our first day together," Felicia continues, "love is blind. Love is blind, and marriage opens your eyes. Do you know that saying, *Marriage is a romance in which the hero dies in the first chapter?* Or, as the French say, *Love is the dawn of marriage, and marriage is the sunset of love.* Sad, but true.

"But there is some consolation. If at first you don't succeed, try, try again. Or, as my friend Eva Gabor says, *Marriage is too interesting an experience to be tried only once or twice.*"

"What's she talking about?" Larry fumes.

"Sounds like she's got it in for marriage." Noah wipes his brow.

"Now, let's review what we've learned:

"We live in a post-Romantic world. Today, orgasms are political. Women are responsible for their orgasms, and men are responsible for theirs. Know what pleases you and go for it. There are times when it's okay to put your needs before the needs of your partner. If you're with a man who has gone off the boil, who doesn't measure up, look around for a replacement.

"Santa," Larry says, reaching under his chair for a thermos, "We're prisoners of war. We're behind enemy lines." The rancher looks across at Noah, pouring himself a steaming cup of whiskey-laced coffee.

Dr. Feingold glances at the two men. She pauses before continuing. "All I'm saying is that we need to protect ourselves. Look after our own interests. What is it about men? We get sexually involved with them and it goes right to our hearts, doesn't it? Women's hearts are generally more open that way. But men have a cut-off valve. Traditionally, it's the woman who is smitten and the man who pulls away. But isn't it better to be heartful than heartless? Better to be smitten than to feel nothing?"

Noah's puzzled. If he sleeps with a woman, it's the woman, likely as not, who shows evidence of having a cut-off valve. And it's Noah who is smitten. Is this un-manly? Un-manly or not, Noah has learned over the years that his susceptibility puts him at a disadvantage. Is he doomed because he lacks a cut-off valve? What if neither men nor women had cut-off valves? What if both felt, and showed that they felt, emotionally involved after the first sexual encounter?

Or maybe it's ornery human nature. If one person's smitten, then the other pulls away. He remembers his father railing at him: "What is it with you? What's this need of yours? You don't have to marry them just because you sleep with them. Do yourself a favor. Do them a favor."

"I adore that woman. Always have," says Larry gesturing at the dyed blonde in the front row. "Yep. What she decides here will make her stay with me or leave. That's what she told me, that's why I'm here. To keep an eye on her."

How long have you been married?"

"Karen and me, we've been together thirty-one years, and I'm not about to start looking for someone new. What about you?

Where's your missus?"

"My wife?"

"Well, unless you've got something going on the side. You are married?"

"Larry, the truth is, my wife just left."

"That so? How long were you married?"

"Ten years."

"Hmm. Too bad. I wonder what the chances are my old lady will stay."

"Shush. Shhh." Hopping down the aisle, a woman sergeant-at-arms scowls and shakes her tennis-tanned fingers in front of Larry's face. She wears Birkenstocks, pink-frosted lipstick and a khaki fanny pack over her abdomen like a L.L. Bean marsupial. Noah takes in the fresh-laundered fragrance of her blue work shirt.

"Gestapo!" he whispers, holding up his hands.

"See, what did I tell you? It's the new master race," Larry moans.

Immediately there's a chorus of shushing from all sides.

"Your support group?" says Noah to the sergeant-at-arms.

"Shush. If you can't keep quiet, leave," says the kangaroo, reaching into her fanny pack for a walky-talky.

"Males," she says to Security. "Yes, I can handle it."

"What are men doing here anyway?" whispers a red-haired woman in the row ahead.

"Spies in the house of love," jokes her seat-mate.

"Good entertainment, but I've had enough!" Noah stands, preparing to leave. "Look, nothing personal, Larry, but I just can't sit still.

"C'mon buddy. Let's hear Dr. Feingold out. I know we're outnumbered, but maybe we'll learn something," Larry whispers, aiming to convince Noah to stay.

Noah figures he is unlikely to be hung for being a spy.

Besides, he feels curiously bonded to Larry, who hands him the coffee mug.

Felicia meanwhile throws back her head so the spotlight can play on her full red lips.

"What can you do to jump-start your new life?" she asks.

Tearing off his jacket, the journalist slumps down in his seat and groans. Divorce, divorce, divorce. If pressed, yes, the writer would confess he's opposed to divorce. Secretly he believes divorced people, himself included, should get back together with their original partners. How's that for inconsistency? How's that for hypocrisy? Larry and his wife of thirty years should stay together. For Noah, the very nature of two people being together is struggle. He can't conceive of anything that doesn't somehow involve struggle—a marriage, researching a feature story, selling a series of articles—maintenance and struggle.

The workshop ends with the women forming a circle and holding hands. One, Priscilla Perkins from Carmel, a goldsmith, invites the group to chant OM, "you know, the universal sound." The room fills with a familiar hum, a sound such as one might hear on a visit to a home video center, the sound of dozens of flickering, but scarcely audible TV sets.

Another begins reading a poem she has written, *Ode To A Two-Hearted Woman*. Mercifully, she is too choked up to get past the first stanza.

Irish psychotherapist, Murphy M., sings a blessing.

> *May the road rise to meet your feet, and may other*
> *good things happen to you, too.*

The women begin a round of applause.

Next, there's a flurry of paper and a hurried exchange of addresses and phone numbers.

Felicia, now more hostess than celebrant, allows her

admirers to come forward for the ritual kissing, hugging and chirruping, those touching gestures and sounds enlightened workshoppers use to convey affection and respect. Some bear gifts for the healer, turquoise jewelry, sticks of incense, drawings, a bouquet of flowers, an envelope containing cash or check. Several women ask for Dr. Feingold's autograph.

"Oh, Felicia, I feel as if I've known you all my life. The time has gone so fast. I'll never forget what I've learned here."

For others, however, the session has been a disappointment. Their faces reveal profound discontent, a sense of something permanently awry, some chronic misery, a sort of terminal neediness.

Finally, half an hour after the big two-hearted doctor's conclusion, the last elated workshopper floats out the door ready, Noah imagines, to walk out on her husband and embrace the challenge of a new life. At last, the turquoise and silver, ceremonial knife-carrying healer perches herself on the flannel-covered massage table. She swings her legs, smiling at Noah. She offers him her hand, which he takes and briefly holds in his own.

"Listen, Dr. Feingold," he begins.

"You can call me Felicia."

He notes the expression in her eyes which seems to say, "Men are fools and I treat them as such, but every now and then I make an exception." She waits for him to speak.

"I just want you to know I'm not someone who makes a habit of this."

"A habit of what?"

"Of phoning up strangers, of talking about my wife with people I don't know."

"And yet you are here."

"Felicia, it's like I told you on the phone," he says, provoked by the twin curvings at the corners of her mouth. "Holly's taken our son and gone off. I'm pissed...I can't sit still."

"What happens when you try?"

"I get jumpy, I keep expecting her to call or pull into the driveway."

Even before she does, he knows she's going to laugh. A bereaved Santa. His cheeks burning, floppy red cap in hand, Noah laughs too.

"Mr. Newmark, tell me, why do you want to be with her?"

"Look, I care for her, I love her and Joey. And, frankly, after five marriages, I don't think I could go through another break up. Jesus, family's important to me or I wouldn't have married so many times. It's crazy, Felicia, but I want to have the experience of one lasting marriage. Can you understand? And something else. I'm against divorce. I think people should just quit fooling around and get back to monogamy. Why are you looking at me like that? I'm contradicting myself, right?"

"You said it, Mr. Newmark, not me."

"Call me Noah. You know, Felicia, I meet someone and learn he—or she—has been married three or four times and I think, What kind of person is this? What's wrong here? And if the person's in a new relationship, right away I'm skeptical. I think, Will it last? Then I remember I've been married five times. There's no accounting for people, is there?"

"What was it like with your ex?"

"She's not my 'ex' yet," he snaps.

"Excuse me, your wife who left with your son."

"Sexually we're okay. At least I think so. We did it the day before she left and, for me anyway, that last time was a good four, maybe five stars. The Golden Kumquat Award. It's true, over the years I've sometimes found it hard to talk to her.

Goddamnit, Felicia, how important is communication anyway?"

"Mr. Newmark, maybe your wife is trying to find herself."

"Holly's been searching for herself for over thirty years, and she doesn't need to change on my account. She's a good mother to our son and, on the whole, I like her just the way she is. But I'm not sure she likes who she is. I'm not sure she likes who she is with me."

"You've been married five times. Well, maybe it hasn't all been in vain. You actually seem quite perceptive. Really, if a casting director chose you to play in a movie version of your life, it wouldn't be believable. Movie critics would call it 'casting against type.' Even apart from that Santa suit, you don't strike me as the garden-variety, much-married man."

"That's comforting. But what can I do to get her back and, if I can't win her back...?"

"What if I told you the cure for a broken heart is you just do it? What if the answer was, Grow a new one? This is going to sound strange, Noah, but the cure for what ails you requires some travel. I'm going to suggest a trip to what folks call the other world."

"The other world?"

"You're thinking, this is bullshit, aren't you?" she says as Noah, grinning, reaches for a glass of water. "Please hear me out."

"I'm looking for guidance," he laughs. "I don't want to insult you, but that sounds ridiculous. What's it going to cost me to go to your other world?"

"I don't set the prices, Noah. My spirit guides do. In order to consult them, you'll need some gold coins."

He puts his hand over his back pocket.

"You have to pay a fee to go to the other world?"

"Of course. In Greek mythology, when the dead arrived, Charon the ferryman had to row them across Acheron's swamp. Remember? And Charon had to be paid an obolos, you know, a penny for the crossing. Those who didn't have a penny became wanderers in the underworld, lost souls."

"Right," Noah says. "That's where the custom of putting a coin in the mouth of a dead person comes from."

"So you do understand," she says, glancing at her watch.

"I hate this...Damn the expense! Okay, Felicia," he says. "I'll give it a try. But...do you know where I can buy some gold coins?"

"I just happen to have some with me," says the healer, displaying a leather pouch.

"Do you take AMERICAN EXPRESS?"

Seeing the look on Felicia's face, he laughs freely for the first time since Holly left.

"I don't accept plastic," says Felicia Feingold.

"I was only joking." Noah pulls out eight twenty-dollar bills. "Will this be enough?"

"Mmm, yeah," Felicia answers.

"Good. Now, can you tell me where I'm going?"

"Let's start with a massage. Just strip down to your shorts and cover up with a towel." She points to a pile of clean, folded towels on a cabinet near the massage table. "Would you like a pillow?" she asks.

"Sure, why not?"

"Now, lie on your back and breathe from your diaphragm. That's right."

Lifting his left leg a few inches off the table, Felicia pulls on it, extending it fully. Then, taking his right foot firmly in her hands, she raises and extends that leg. She devotes two or three minutes to each leg.

"That feels good, but what are you trying to do?" Noah asks, opening his eyes.

"We store experiences in our bodies. Some experiences cause imbalances, knots or blockages, which can result in dis-ease.

Really, I'm just a channel, a facilitator whose job it is to help people in the process..."

"Process? What process?"

"Let's just say it's subtler and more powerful than acupuncture.

She rubs and squeezes each of his toes before going on to work her thumbs into the balls of his feet. He watches as she chafes her hands, then presses and works her fingers over what she calls 'pulses' on his legs and sides.

"Just relax now and follow the in-flow and out-flow of your breath," she says, both hands on his chest.

"By the way, Noah, in the future you need to work more on blockages around your heart. You're definitely tight there." She raps with her fingers to show him where she means.

"Next, you're going to visualize where you're going, and what you're going to do, in the other world," she says.

"Where am I going?" Noah asks.

"Your destination is Second Chance Mesa," she says, touching his mouth. "Everything important in life involves a horizontal surface. A desk, bed, table top or altar. You know what the word *mesa* means, don't you?"

"*Mesa* means table," Noah answers. "Mesas are elevated and they have flat tops."

"That's right. Mesas are like altars. My teacher says mesas are sacred places."

"What's next?" Noah asks.

"Next you need a mental picture, a map of where you're going." Again, she raises his head with one hand and presses the 'pulses' in his neck with the other.

"A mental map of Second Chance Mesa?" he says, as his eyes roll up and come to a point of focus between his eyebrows.

"That's right," she says.

"What's going on?" he asks.

"Tell me what you're feeling," says Felicia.

"My eyes are pulsating."

"Pulsating?" Felicia asks.

"I close them," Noah explains, "and they roll up..."

"Your vision—your eyes—are becoming one. That's a sign your third eye is opening. You can see from inside now, can't you? Good," she says. "Now, relax. No matter what happens, experience your emotions and feelings as if you were seeing them on a movie screen."

A light breeze sweeps across his face. Still on his back, Noah, his eyes rotating, glides backward into space. He has the sensation of leaving his body and, at the same time, taking it with him. As he continues rising, he looks back to see himself dozing on the flannel-covered table.

"Before we go on," he hears Felicia say, "you must forgive Holly and the others for leaving."

"I don't think I can do that," he says.

"The question is, can you let go of the drama?"

"Drama?" Noah asks.

"Yes, drama. Whether they left you or you left them, you somehow managed to say 'I quit' before those unfortunate women could say, 'You're fired.' How do we know you didn't set it up so along the way even those women who didn't want to leave you were forced to leave?

"And in doing so you abandoned your children..."

"Okay, Felicia, I forgive...I forgive them all," he says.

"Don't you think you better ask them for forgiveness?"

"You mean in person? What do you expect me to do?" Noah asks.

"Right now all you have to do is settle things in yourself. You can forgive them later in person if you want."

"Hey, what did you do with it, Felicia?" he asks.

"With what?" she says, her voice rising.

"With my body, where's my body?" he asks, looking right and left.

"It'll be with you when you land. Do you see a place to land?"

He looks down upon what appears to be an island made of sandstone—several miles in length and a mile wide.

"I see the sky and some clouds. Everything's the same color," he says. "Everything's buff-colored, yellow."

"Okay, okay," she sighs. "When you're ready to land, you'll see a river on one side of the Mesa. That's the River of Forgiveness and it'll be to your right as you approach."

"I see it now. And a red-tailed hawk."

Felicia applies pressure to pulses near his kidneys and shoulders. The left side of his body begins to vibrate slightly under her touch.

"I've just landed. It's very sandy," he says.

"Do you know the story of Johnny Lone Soul?" she asks.

"Johnny Lone Soul? No," he says.

"Okay, I'm going to tell you. Follow Johnny Lone Soul on his journey to Second Chance Mesa."

"Johnny Lone Soul?"

"Just listen." Felicia runs her fingers over Noah's forehead. "Johnny Lone Soul had his heart broken so many times by so many women, he had to get a new heart. So one morning, after many sleepless nights, Johnny went to see his grandmother. Grandmother told him, 'At the first light of dawn, take your heart and go to the world of Second Chance Mesa. When you get there, throw your heart away. Throw it into the River of Forgiveness.

"'Then,' said Grandmother, 'in order to grow a new heart you must find a stone the same size as your heart. Put the stone into a leather pouch and carry it in your shirt pocket for as long as it takes for it to break into pieces.'

"'Every morning, at dawn, you must go to Second Chance Mesa. Dip the stone in the River of Forgiveness and let it soften. Each day, after you have washed your stone, put it back in its pouch and carry the pouch in your pocket.

"'Only in that way will the stone soften.'

"Everything in you hardens into stone," she explains. "People do not die of a broken heart. They die of other parts of themselves calcifying into stone. Dipping your stone in water washes away bitterness and anger.

"Of course, Grandmother watched as the stone softened. When all the sorrow and bitterness had gone out of it, Grandmother said, 'It's time to give me the pouch.' And Johnny Lone Soul gave her the pouch.

"So much time had gone by and the stone had been washed and worn and handled so many times that it had broken into little pieces. In fact, the pouch was filled with tiny pebbles.

"Grandmother said, 'Now, what do you suppose I have in my hand?' And Johnny Lone Soul watched as Grandmother, with a touch, changed what had been stone into a human heart and pressed it into Johnny's chest.

"That's how Johnny Lone Soul got his new heart."

Tapping Noah's shoulder, Felicia smiles as he stretches and yawns.

"As for you, my friend, you paid up in gold. Truly, you know how to journey to the other world and can go there whenever you choose. From now on you're going to do as Johnny Lone Soul did until the spirit guide says you've accomplished your task."

Suddenly Noah sees Holly and Joey. Holly's smiling and

ice-skating with their son on a frozen pond. In the vision she's crying, "It's done. It's done."

"What's done?" Scratching his head, Noah stands. Felicia hands him his Santa jacket. As she does so, she reaches into one of the pockets and pulls out a fist-sized chunk of sandstone. Taking Noah's hand, she places the rock in his palm and closes his fingers around it.

8

The Bamboo Egg Roll

In no hurry to return to Mt. Chakra, he stops in Watsonville at the Bamboo Egg Roll. Noah and Holly had eaten at the Egg Roll a week before on Joey's birthday. Other times they made the trip to get away from Mt. Chakra's stir-fried veggies and tofu-burgers.

Seated at a table for two, Noah discovers a Chinese fortune cookie left behind from a previous diner. Believing fortune cookies should be handed out at the beginning of a meal rather than at the end—to warn one in advance of contaminated shellfish, for example, or a careless chef—he breaks open the cookie. If the prediction is bad, he'll walk out of the restaurant and dine at Fondue Fred's.

"Happy news is on the way," says the cookie.

Noah takes that to mean he'll have a decent lunch. He orders hot and sour soup, and shrimp with almonds and snow peas. To drink? Budweiser.

While waiting for lunch, he picks up the *Watsonville Gazette*. Reads the Astrology column. Holly is a Capricorn, ruthlessly stubborn and narrow minded. Noah muses over the fact he's been married to her for ten years, longer than to any of the others. Yet she's the wife with whom he is most incompatible. She's a devotee of Los Angeles glamour and the show biz party scene. Theatrical bullshit. In contrast, he's a loner, either grading papers or writing his heart out. Compared to Holly, Noah broods, he's practically a recluse. At home after one of her ten-hour days at the studio, she's filled with breathless gossip, behind-the-scenes, soap opera blippity blop. For his part, he longs to tell her about his stories and share what he's discovered about the words he's looked up in the dictionary.

Although she's his opposite, he feels some inexplicable draw, an almost indecent need to please and see her happy. "Imagine being obsessed with your wife! Cool it, Noah. Cool it or you'll lose her," Shelley Levine advised. Noah did what he could to play hard to get. Off and on over the years he tried to feign coolness, indifference, but couldn't make it stick. A few days of well-intentioned indifference and all he could think of was holding Holly again in his arms.

He misses her. He misses the Shalimar and make-up powder, the palette of juices, the taste of her orange blossom bosom, her effervescence, the ache in his heart, the pain in the ass. That's what she was, a pain in the ass. He misses the pearly silk outfit she wore to bed that first night and the lace dress with the puff sleeves she had on when they met and the little–tiny they seemed– pink shoes with straps held on by a pearl button that she later invited him to undo. "Undo me," she said. "I do, yes, darling, I do," he said.

Phoning his first wife, he'd complain, "Okay, Shelley, I'm uxorious. Five wives and I'm suddenly irrationally devoted to one. Can I help it? Not that I didn't adore you, too. Don't misunderstand."

"So what's the great attraction?" Shelley wanted to know.

Noah kept his mouth shut. What was he supposed to say? "Because I love the hellion."

Two weeks after their wedding, still honeymooning, they dined at a Chinese restaurant, O'Mei Happy Garden ("No MSG").

Holly, assuming the role of one Chinese Fortune Cookie talking to another, remarked, *A dream need not fade in the light.*

To which Noah, talking Fortune Cookie, replied, *Someone special is secretly in love with you.*

The position you desire will soon be yours, said Holly, egg roll in hand. *Women appreciate men who can perform duet.*

Your ability to believe has created a dream-come-true, responded *Noah, veteran of many such* fortunes.

To take advantage of an opportunity, you must first recognize it, Holly joked, reaching for a prawn with her chop sticks.

I'm glad we speak the same language.

Recalling their honeymoon, his eyes fill. Reaching into his pocket for notebook and pen, Noah turns back to the Gazette.

And what is Holly's horoscope today?

"The structure of oppression will be smashed," says the astrologer, "and your shining crystal of truth will be revealed for all to see."

Next he looks at his own. "Leo the lion: forget love entanglements. Practice charity."

A moment later he's raging. "Charity? I should feel charity for Holly! Someone who, with no preamble, leaves and kidnaps six-year-old Joey?"

Across the aisle, two gray-haired women dressed in blue jogging suits are reminiscing. Noah eavesdrops.

"I know how you feel. About twelve years ago just when I was ready to leave Herb, he did the funniest thing. He began taking guitar lessons and would serenade me. I remember he'd sing...Ain't no sunshine when you're gone. Funny. And it all worked out."

It worked for that woman's husband. Why not for him? Why

not guitar lessons? Why not serenade Holly? Why not win her back with music?

"Guitar lessons? Horoscopes? Love doctors? Newmark, you're really going off the deep end."

9

Waiting to See the Silent One

Mt. Chakra

DECEMBER 23

Noah stays up all night scribbling in his notebook, drinking beer and watching television. In spite of its rating—"pure fertilizer"—he watches director Ed Adlum's *Invasion of the Blood Farmers* about some modern-day Druids. He watches Jay Raskin's *I Married A Vampire* ("better than Sominex") and Paul Mazursky's *Bob & Carol & Ted & Alice* with Elliot Gould and Dyan Cannon ("lots of funny moments").

Squinty-eyed, tongue swollen, face flushed, he wakes to a raucous cawing, *caw, caw,* a reveille of crows. Stumbling to the bathroom, tripping over one of Joey's worn-out sneakers, he hallucinates. A cataclysmic event has occurred and, apparently, he has been left behind—left to die?—by those who escaped.

Wake up. Get with it.

What are his choices?

Choice 1—*The macho approach:* He can go one-on-one with the Champion of Living. Keeping his appointment, pretending all is right with the world, he can interview the man as scheduled.

Choice 2—*The I-have-a-headache approach:* He can postpone the interview "for personal reasons," complaining, "I'm ready to jump out of my skin. Up all night with fever and chills, could I have a rain check?"

Choice 3—*The mad man approach:* He can begin breaking and burning furniture in the best zombie-beast tradition.

7:00 A.M.

Pelted by rain, Noah makes his way to the Volvo to pick up a fresh notepad and file of background notes. He tosses these into a briefcase and runs through a grove of redwood trees. Five minutes later, he approaches the circular corrugated metal building. "Welcome to Mt. Chakra. Administration Office."

Relieved to have reached this familiar structure, recalling the nature of his mission, but seeing two of everything, including two blurry, wet door bells, he rings one. Concentrating on keeping his eyes from rolling, ready to enunciate every syllable with care, he waits for the woman known as Anandi Joy.

"Noah, you're here early. Here, let me help you. Come in, come in," says the physician's white-clad, 180-pound secretary. Funny how many of the women at Mt. Chakra are solidly built, powerhouses of raw energy. At 6'2", Noah towers over immaculately groomed Anandi Joy (formerly Sandra Rothchild), but guesses his weight is about the same as hers. On the other hand, the men at Mt. Chakra are lean and ascetic looking. Does the practice of yoga create some substance in these women that it doesn't create in the men?

"I was hoping for a little extra time with Rama."

"I'm sorry, Noah, but unless there's a cancellation, I don't think that's possible. You do have a couple hours as it is. You know what morning's are like for him."

"This is no ordinary morning."

"Really? What does that mean?"

"This is a big day for me. I've never interviewed someone who doesn't talk."

"Would you like a cup of tea while you're waiting?"

"No, thanks, but I could do with something nourishing. How about a cup of coffee?"

"You're in luck. I just happen to have a jar of instant. And here's the honey. You do look stressed," she says, handing him a cup.

"Noah, I've been thinking: maybe you should ask him more about why he doesn't talk."

"My wife Holly asked him that."

"She did?"

"Yeah, 'How can I stop talking so much?' she asked. Actually she was asking about herself."

"And what did Rama answer?"

"He wrote on his little chalkboard: I TOO ONCE ASKED MYSELF THAT QUESTION. Then he erased those words and wrote, I STOPPED TALKING. My hunch is that, like Holly, he too was once a talker. My guess is that talking was the thing he loved doing most and that he gave it up because that was the hardest thing for him to do.

"My wife says talking with him is like having a conversation with a Chinese fortune cookie."

Anandi turns to pluck dead leaves off a poinsettia plant.

Thirty minutes later, in a moment of weakness, Noah changes his mind about doing the interview. Reaching for his car keys, he prepares to drive to Santa Cruz. He needs to talk, he needs someone to listen. He thinks of his grandmother who used to tell how, in Russia, village women in distress would run out of their homes into the street and bang on a tea kettle—*hok a chainik*—until all their friends would gather around them.

"Oy, boubala, boubala, why are you banging on that kettle?"

"Oh, that husband of mine. He wants this and that and he never lets me alone." And more than half a century later, the Yiddish expression had evolved into its modern meaning of *endless complaining*, Noah reflects.

Why not jump in his station wagon and head for the lounge of the nearest bar? Order a morning margarita? Sip tequila and lemon juice, bang with a spoon on the icy salted glass and shout for help?

Five minutes later, he changes his mind again. Why not use himself as a guinea pig? Why not tell the doctor what's really on his mind? Why not put Rama and himself to a test of sorts? Who's to say? Such a conversation might come in handy for the feature. Oh, yes, the feature.

He pulls out a spiral notebook and begins:

- Born in Israel, Anandi Joy is a Berkeley-educated lawyer. Diplomatic trouble-shooter, sentry and earth mother.

- Why is it that passionate people (Anandi Joy) so often turn out to be spiritual seekers?

- Vital facts, names, ages, dates, relationships of people at mountain top retreat? Interview Anandi.
  Ask her: where do new devotees come from and why?
  How are visitors welcomed? Cost of room and board?
  Daily practice? What's required?
  Special events? Holidays?

- Unimpeded views. Mt. Chakra. The topside of winter fog. What it's like to look down on cloud cover. Waking in a tent. Redwood tree shadow. Deer foraging for food. The tool shop, storage shed & geraniums. Whole families camping out in hobbit huts covered with bougainvillea. Swimming in a mountain lake near Admin. Bldg. Late model Volvos, Toyotas and Mercedes in parking lot (gravel) near the commune high school.

- A rich people yoga country club. True or false?

- 'Enough is enough.' It is also said 'Enough is too much.' At what point did the people at Mt. Chakra say 'Enough is enough'? Or did they ask themselves, "Is that all there is?" Was it divine revelation, inspiration, or epiphany that made them seek out a 101-year-old East Indian physician? Or were they simply sick and tired of being sick and tired? Or, or...

• What of those who come and get disillusioned?

And what about this Sandra Rothchild who, eyes bright, smelling of incense and the commune's chai—a blend of black tea, cinnamon, cardamom, nutmeg and cloves—has clearly been up since dawn? Anyone at Mt. Chakra who, at 7 A.M., smells of East Indian chai and sandalwood, has probably already showered, meditated for an hour and had a light breakfast.

What is her function here? In researching the story, Noah learned that some yogis, like corporate CEO's, have administrative assistants to protect them from unwelcome visitors. Sandra Rothchild, thirty-something aide to the Champion of Living, once worked as a lawyer for a San Francisco law firm. At Mt. Chakra she serves as a gatekeeper, determining who will and will not get to see Rama. Even as he waits, she answers the phone, sets up appointments. Noah laughs as, between calls, she grinds tumeric and sandalwood powder into a paste.

"What's that for?" Noah asks.

"First aid for acne, for the teenagers who live here. It's an old prescription. It's combined with half a cup of aloe vera juice twice a day."

"The doctor practices Ayurvedic medicine."

"Good for you. You read those books I gave you."

"Pulse diagnosis? Healing oils? Enemas? It's not for me, Joy."

"Well, of Ayurveda's mind-body types yours is right on. *Pitta*: reddish complexion with freckles, high energy, quick-tempered..."

Noah decides she might possibly have healing powers of her own.

"Joy, I hear you grew up in Israel."

"That's right."

"And that you worked on a *kibbutz.*"

"Right again, Noah. What are you, a private eye?" she asks.

"I'm a writer. I'm supposed to do this. Look, I know I sound pushy, but what is your exact title?"

"I don't have one."

"You have a law degree. What made you leave a *kibbutz*, and then a law practice, for Mt. Chakra?"

"None of your business," snaps the former Sandra Rothchild.

Again the phone rings. Standing, she answers it and, a moment later, hangs up.

Now she focuses on the journalist.

"There are people here who would like to read your article. Before it's published. You understand. We want to be sure the facts are straight. We have total confidence in you..."

"But...?"

"Rightly or wrongly, communities like ours are in disfavor. Remember Bhagwan Shree Rajneesh, that free sex *macher* in Oregon? Any time anyone writes about healers or yoga teachers, that's what people think of. People on the outside are ready to believe the worst.

"We've given you all the background information you asked for," says Anandi, her hands on her hips. "We'll continue to cooperate, but now we'd like you to cooperate."

Noah sobers up.

"I've been here three weeks and now, before this key interview, you've got some new conditions. What the hell are you pulling on me?"

"Take it or leave it, Mr. Newmark," Anandi says.

"Does Rama know what you're up to? You'll see the finished story when it's published. No journalist shows his work to the people he writes about. For approval. What you're asking is unethical. I'm not in the business of writing press releases."

"No one is asking for a press release. This is a complex story, and you told us you have a deadline. There's room for error and we're offering to help you get the facts straight."

"There's always a deadline. But I have an editor and people at the magazine whose job it is to check facts. We talked about this on the phone. Didn't you agree then? This isn't the first article I've written."

"Take it easy. I know I gave you the go-ahead. It's probably my fault. Now I've been overruled by others on the Board—not Rama. Yes, people in communes vie for power, too. The problem is the commune, and Rama himself, have more to lose by this than you do. So we may have to withdraw permission for the interview. Besides, Rama doesn't need anyone to write about him. It's not as if he needs to recruit more people to heal. He's probably the only doctor in America who acts on the belief that there's a contradiction between taking money from people and healing them. In fact, he says the more money a doctor takes from a patient, the longer it takes for the patient to heal. And that taking money from poor people shortens their time on earth, and diminishes the life, the spiritual life, of the doctor."

"Why does he heal people?"

"Because the first principle of medicine is compassion."

"Compassion?"

"The doctor calls it *sympathetic consciousness*."

"Why would he bother to see me?"

"Is it possible that you, like the rest of us, are in need of some 'sympathetic consciousness'? Noah, remember, you asked to see him. The *Champion of Living* story idea came from you. I asked around, I'm being candid, and learned you have a reputation for staying away from sleaze. At a time when communities like ours are under scrutiny, if not attack, I thought you could be useful to us.

And that maybe you could benefit personally. I like the work of yours I've read. That's the truth."

"Sandra, if it turns out you like the article, fine. But no one reads what I write before it goes to the editor."

"God, you're stubborn. Other Board members are going to ask. You know that."

"They're free to ask. I've dealt with power plays before. And you're right. It's your fault. Whether you intended to or not, you set me up. But I have an idea. Why don't we let the doctor decide? I'll ask him. If he says show the article to you for approval, I'll do it."

East or West, doctors are doctors. What they enjoy doing more than anything else, the journalist decides, is making people wait. Noah uses the time to look over his notes. He re-reads D.T. Matthews' description of Rama in *The Voice of Silence*. Matthews visited Rama in Bombay in the 1960s. "He's tall and lanky, but this ascetic 160-pound physician architecturally designed and helped build the laboratories and clinics...He sleeps four hours a night. His food intake for the last thirty years has been fruit, vegetables and eight cups of water a day...yet when there's no other way of moving a support beam or slab of concrete, Indian construction workers call him. Like a character in a TV cartoon, he lifts heavy objects with one-pointedness of mind."

Noah wonders if he read something like that years ago in *Be Here Now*. Conceivably Rama's power is equal to that of other noted teachers.

Struggling to stay awake, Noah thrashes around in his seat, bites his lips, opens his eyes as wide as he can. Shuts them. And again opens them.

Joy floats two feet off the floor. She and the half-lit office whirl like dervishes. Obsessed with *The Champion of Living,* Noah decides to include a muscular, white-clad, 180-pound woman—who levitates. He'll also include this Quonset hut office with its bouquet of chrysanthemums, Indian prints and a shrine to some six-limbed dancing deity. And the women at the commune, women in 60s' style granny dresses and work boots, women wearing layered skirts and babushkas—like boubas in some 19th Century Russian *shetl.*

If he can just get into his writer mode, he'll be okay. The journalist strains to become the journalist.

"Sandra, come on. You ran a background check on me. Now I'd like to ask you a few questions."

"Why me?"

"As I see it, you're an important part of this story. Besides, I'm curious about how you got here. Let's say I'm a nosey journalist. I'd like to know why you left the *kibbutz.*"

"Why? Because in Israel religion and politics are too tied up with one another. There's no room for idealism. If you haven't been there, you don't know what it's like. For me there was something missing. I'm one of those people who needs some sort of ideal. Mt. Chakra is my *kibbutz.*

"So, the short answer to your question is: here I feel fulfilled. Living on a *kibbutz* I didn't."

"What about that San Francisco law firm?"

"I only worked there for a year."

Sandra Rothchild goes back to concocting Ayurvedic prescriptions. Licorice and ginger tea for asthma. One teaspoon honey and one-eighth teaspoon black pepper for breathlessness.

"What do you have for a nervous stomach?"

Sandra mixes the juice of half a lemon with a pinch of baking soda. Adding water, she hands the drink to Noah.

Moments later he exclaims, "My God, it works!"

"What else do you want to know?" she asks, dropping a sugar cube into a vase filled with roses. "In case you're wondering, fresh-cut flowers like sugar. A little sugar makes them stay fresh longer because it kills the fungi that attack the flowers."

"If you say so. Tell me, Sandra, does Rama perform marriages? Someone told me he's a Universal Life minister. Does that mean he marries people?"

"Already you're thinking of re-marrying? Sorry, I couldn't resist. He used to."

"He used to? What happened?"

"Some of the couples he married got divorced. Where he comes from that's not supposed to happen."

"People at Mt. Chakra get divorced?"

"Your middle name is divorce. You're surprised?"

"I'd like to think there's somewhere, Mt. Chakra say, where people don't get divorced."

The intercom clicks on. Noah hears a light tapping sound.

"He'll see you in ten minutes."

Fidgeting, pacing up and back like an expectant father, Noah breaks into a sweat. He has his notes, his outline, a list of questions. Weeks ago, at Silver Screen College, he lectured, "There's no story without background, no story without thorough research, no story without focus."

He knows what he wants from the interview. But Noah is superstitious. A creature of habit. He runs through a little ritual before every interview. As he has done for twenty years, he shuts his eyes and repeats his mantras:

1. Marshall's Generalized Iceberg Theorem: ⅞ of everything is invisible.

2. Life is an onion. Peel away the layers.

3. The enemy is passivity. The enemy is gullibility. Wake up!

And his questions. Noah does all he can to come up with questions that are short and to the point. He is not always successful.

1. Doctor, what is the goal of yoga?

2. What's the connection between the practice of yoga and healing?

3. What is the function of a master?

4. Who has benefited more, the yogis and teachers who have raided the West for money and power, or the West's spiritual materialists who have raided the East for wisdom and peace of mind?

5. Last weekend you had an evening program of Irish folk songs, dancing and theater. What was that all about?

6. This place is called Mt. Chakra. Why? What is a chakra?

7. What advice do you have for people who want to live 100 years?

8. Why are you silent?

10

Marriage #1
Much-Married Man Tells All

8:00 A.M.

Rama P. Rama lives in a three-room, bougainvillea-covered redwood cabin behind the Administration Building. Leaving his Birkenstocks in the hallway, Noah looks around for the physician. He peers into the bedroom. No one there. He glances into the kitchen with its stainless steel counter tops. No one there.

Noah hears a whispered "*Pssst.*"

Turning, he sees Rama in his living room. The doctor is seated on a sofa facing a 32-inch console TV. Deciding to include this detail later in his *Our Times Magazine* feature, the journalist stands in the doorway mentally constructing his lead. Noah visualizes the title, *The Champion of Living*, photographs of the commune, and his opening paragraph.

> Rama has a long white beard, reddish-brown skin and has never been married. He is 101 years old, but looks youthful, like an unusually tall East Indian snake charmer with prematurely gray hair. He goes barefoot and wears a long, loose white cotton shirt and Indian pajama trousers. He's nearsighted and, when he isn't using them, his glasses, attached to a thin black cord, dangle from his neck.

What would he say about that as a journalism instructor?

"What's your angle? What's this story about? Punch it up. Re-write with more action and less description."

As a teacher, Noah decides, he has something to offer. Does he dare give up teaching before he makes a comeback?

"Pssst."

The physician motions for Noah to enter and sit beside him. The TV set is off, but there's a current *Guide* and a remote control device by the doctor's knee. Noah sits a few inches away from the channel switcher. Does the Champion of Living watch *Good Morning America? Donohue? My Many Children?*

Noah has a device of his own: a voice-activated micro-cassette recorder.

"Do you mind if I use this thing?" he asks.

Rama points to his mouth and beams as if to say, "It doesn't matter to me."

Noah presses the record button. Each time the physician writes something on his chalkboard, Noah plans to read it back to him. That way he'll have a record of his own questions and Rama's replies.

Noah's puzzled. How come the doctor's so agreeable? In Noah's experience, everyone's on the make, everyone wants something. And if Rama wants something there's going to be a subtext. What's the subtext?

Taking his place on the sofa, scarcely looking at the page, he writes,

> Rama's skin is smooth, like a young man's....the dull, brown richness of fine-baked, whole grain bread fresh out of an oven...Still, there is something about him of the aged, wizened Siddhartha, the aristocratic, classically handsome jungle sadhu.

"Oh, come off it!" exclaims Noah's inner critic.

Noah tries again.

> Journalist William Shirer once said of his interviews
> with Gandhi in the 1930s, 'You felt you were the
> only person in the room, that he had all the time in
> the world for you.' This is true of Dr. R.

Gesturing at bowls filled with apples and almonds and another brimming with chocolates, the doctor encourages Noah to help himself.

"This place is called Mt. Chakra. Why? What is a *chakra*?" Noah asks, peeling tinfoil from a Hershey kiss.

SANSKRIT WORD. CAKRAM MEANS WHEEL, Rama writes. CHAKRAS—SPIRITUAL ENERGY CENTERS ON SPINAL COLUMN AND IN THE HEAD. PURPOSE OF YOGA IS TO AWAKEN CHAKRAS.

"Why?"

FOR INNER PEACE AND UNION WITH GOD.

"God? God who?"

Mirroring the writer's expression, Rama writes, GOD THE FATHER. ADONAI. YHVH. YAHWEH.

"You went to yeshiva? You studied the Talmud?"

Compressing his lips, sighing, Rama shrugs like an old rabbi.

JEWS COME TO MT. CHAKRA. GOYIM STUDY AT YESHIVA.

Keeping pace with the doctor, Noah speedwrites Rama's answers word for word.

"Okay, I've got another question. Who has benefited more, the yogis and teachers who raided the West for money and power, or the West's spiritual materialists who raided the East for wisdom and peace of mind?

"Excuse me a moment," he says, pressing the Rewind button. He plays back the tape to see if it's recording.

Rama writes on the chalkboard, YOU READ. YOU INTERVIEW PEOPLE. WHAT DO YOU THINK?

"The spiritual materialists from the West get something, and the snatch-and-grab teachers from the East get something too. No offense intended. Anyway, I think it all evens out.

"By the way, speaking of masters, speaking of teachers, what is the function of a master?" Noah asks.

"*Ssst,*" says Rama. That *Ssst* sound, Noah realizes, is Rama's way of laughing. He puts on his bifocals and writes, THE FUNCTION OF A MASTER IS TO SHOW THE PATH AND LEAVE.

Noah pops another chocolate in his mouth.

"So you don't collect disciples," he finds himself saying. At the same time, he rummages through his notes for his next question.

"Last weekend you had an evening program given over entirely to Irish folk songs, dancing and theater. What was that all about?"

YOGA POSTURES KEEP BODY FLEXIBLE AND STRONG, the doctor writes. FOLK SONGS, DANCING, PLAYS DO THE SAME. YOUR BAAL SHEM TOV DANCED AND SANG AS A FORM OF WORSHIP. WHO TEACHES THAT GOD IS OPPOSED TO JOY?

"So you have music and dance from all over the world here?" Rama nods.

"I understand you're 101 years old," Noah says. "What advice do you have for people who want to live to be a hundred?"

I DON'T KNOW. IT'S OUT OF MY HANDS, Rama writes.

Noah laughs. "Some old people recommend a shot of whiskey every day, a little marijuana, a garlic clove—"

OLD PEOPLE? WHAT'S OLD? YOUR METHUSELAH LIVED 969 YEARS.

"My Methuselah?"

The journalist scratches his head. "I seem to be asking the wrong questions. Maybe I should come back later..." Then he notices something odd about the doctor's eyes, and writes:

> Rama's left eye shines with welcome, but his right
> appears cold, dead to the world.

Rama inclines his head and reads what his interviewer has written.

PAUL KLEE SAYS, 'ONE EYE SEES, THE OTHER FEELS,' he writes on his chalkboard.

Noah writes in his notebook:

> An artist himself, he attracts artists.
>
> Seventeen years ago Catherine K., a painter, visited Rama and asked, "How can I combine spiritual practice with my work as an artist?"
>
> BECOME ART, he wrote on his chalkboard.
>
> That was all Catherine needed. She continued with her spiritual discipline and work for seventeen years. Then she went to see him a second time.
>
> Recalling their first encounter, he wrote, DID YOU UNDERSTAND WHAT I MEANT?

"In front of you I don't know whether to close my eyes or keep them open," says Noah.

WHY DON'T YOU LET ME ALONE AND MEDITATE ON YOURSELF?

"Huh? What's that you said?"

LET'S GO ON, the doctor writes.

"Who are you?" Noah asks.

I USED TO KNOW.

"And now?"

Rama shrugs.

"What I mean is, say language made it possible for you to give people a further sense of who you are. Not just you, but any person. Can someone say in language who they are?"

IF I HAVE TO EXPRESS MYSELF, I CAN'T DO IT THROUGH TALKING. TO TASTE A SWEET, YOU HAVE TO TASTE IT, the doctor writes.

Noah speedwrites:

> In other words, he doesn't describe himself as a person, or use his history to do this for him. He

doesn't define himself by the work he does. He doesn't say, for example, 'I am a doctor.' Who he is, he says, is his experience.

"So how can I write about you? How can I write about anyone? Is it even possible?"

EXPERIENCE IS NECESSARY. BECOME WHAT YOU DESCRIBE AND THEN WRITE ABOUT IT.

"What are you saying? I have to become you in order to have your experience? I have to have your experience in order to write about you?"

A PAINTING OF FIRE LOOKS LIKE FIRE, BUT IT CAN'T BURN, the doctor writes. IT IS A DEPICTION OF FIRE.

"So I'm supposed to become a 'silent one,' a 101-year-old East Indian physician...? You know, if I do as you say, I'll end up being your brother. Wouldn't that be something! Are you suggesting I trash this *Champion of Living* article and, instead, write our autobiography?"

BEGIN BY BEING SILENT ONE DAY A WEEK.

Rama peels and slices an apple. He offers half to Noah who, nibbling, writes:

> While it's true the doctor's cut out one level of communication in choosing to remain silent, he's added another by allowing each word he prints on the chalkboard to be recorded and pondered.
>
> He's precise, as one would expect a physician to be. He won't allow mis-readings or fuddled interpretations of what he puts on his chalkboard.

"By the way, what made you take a vow of silence?" Half way into the question, Noah bites his tongue. He already has the answer in his notes.

YOU KNOW. IT KEEPS ME OUT OF ARGUMENTS.

"Okay, okay. And what is...what do you think makes a cult?"

Noah asks, checking the tape counter.

WHEN PEOPLE FEEL WHAT IS BEST FOR THEM IS BEST FOR OTHERS TOO.

"What about political parties? I mean, what about politicians who think they know what's right for other people?"

"Ssssst..."

"Okay, sir, changing the subject, tell me, how are we supposed to live our lives?"

HUFF AND PUFF AND PRETEND IT MATTERS, Rama writes.

Noah laughs. "Okay, then, let's talk about death...What is..."

JOURNEY FORWARD, Rama writes.

"Journey forward? That's death?"

NOBODY DIES A MOMENT TOO LATE OR A MOMENT TOO SOON.

"Is that a whip or a fan?" Noah asks, his attention falling on a cluster of blue-green feathers in an umbrella stand. "What do you do with those?"

PEACOCK FEATHERS = FRUITFULNESS. BESTOW BLESSING.

"Oh, yeah," he says, recalling Anandi's account of how Rama sometimes rapped people with his 'wand,' striking them, the writer imagined, in the manner of a queen or king bestowing knighthood.

ARE YOU AT PEACE? Rama writes.

"Hell no. This disinterested journalist stuff is a charade," he says. "Anyway, I'm supposed to be asking the questions. I'm interviewing you."

YOU CAN SAY WHAT'S ON YOUR MIND, the doctor writes.

"Okay, I'm grateful," Noah says. "I appreciate your willingness to see me. It's actually kind of funny talking to you, a man who's gone a hundred years without getting married."

The doctor waits for Noah to continue.

"My wife Holly has taken Joey and run off—I think with another man."

Dear God. Noah can hardly believe what he's hearing himself say. These lips, which for ten years had kissed her mouth, licked and nuzzled her body, saying, 'Another man...'

"I've been wifeless for three days...a week...I've lost track of time."

The writer struggles to keep from leaning back on the sofa. Working to keep his eyes focused, he has about him the air of an earthquake victim just emerged from rubble. What did he bring his family here for anyway? Why here? Why did it have to happen here, on Mt. Chakra?

A *mauni sadhu,* a monk who has practiced continual silence for more than 50 years, the doctor is, at this moment, in a sweetly reasonable, if altered, state. Or so he appears to Noah.

"Okay, doctor, now you're the interviewer. We've reversed roles. What do you want to know?"

HOW MANY TIMES MARRIED? Rama writes on the 8" x 10" chalkboard dangling from his belt.

"Mmm, more than once," Noah answers.

HOW MANY CHILDREN?

"Doctor, the Biblical Noah only had one wife. I've been husband to more than two. More than three."

HOW MANY TIMES MARRIED? writes the doctor, rapping on the chalkboard.

"How many times married?" Noah says. "Five arks. In Chicago, where I was born, they have a zoo. The Ark in Lincoln Park they call it."

SO, FIVE MARRIAGES. HOW MANY CHILDREN?

"How many children? Four," he answers, scratching his head.

"You know, I'm having trouble getting used to being the interviewee."

The doctor shrugs his shoulders and draws some lines, makes a diagram on his chalkboard:

MARRIAGE	WIFE	CHILDREN	CITY
1			
2			
3			
4			
5			

HOW MANY CHILDREN WITH MARRIAGE ONE? he wants to know.

"None with one." Noah rubs his eyes. How could Holly do it? How could she leave him like that without saying anything? Just a few scribbled words pinned to the pillow.

WHERE LIVING? the doctor writes, and shows the chalkboard to Noah.

"Shelley, my first, lives in Chicago."

MARRIAGE TWO? The doctor pokes sharply at the board with a 3-inch chalkstick mounted in a steel holder. Noah yawns and scratches, unable to concentrate. His mouth feels hot and dry as baked sandpaper. His muscles ache and, at the same time, he feels like moving, like swimming or playing tennis. The silent one pokes again at the board. He's demanding an answer.

MARRIAGE TWO? The doctor continues tapping with the chalkstick. "Two children," he mumbles. "Jim and Carol."

WHERE LIVING? asks the doctor.

"Where living?" Noah repeats the question.

"Boulder, Colorado."

Anna. He married Anna as he might have entered a movie theater, encouraged by the reviews ("Classy family entertainment," "Anna Jones is outstanding!"), with a certain longing for sensation ("not to be missed," "a romantic adventure that will stir your heart") and, shameful confession, with the idea that if ever he found himself bored or restless he could always get up and leave. Shameful. Shameful stuff.

MARRIAGE THREE? writes Rama.

"One child. New York. Manhattan. Ariel. I'm Ariel's father—this year Ariel's spending the holidays with her mother.

"You know, this is harder than going through a divorce. But there's a lesson in this, isn't there, doctor? You're holding up a kind of mirror—or a chalkboard—to my life. I'm glad this isn't the day of reckoning. I'm glad I'm still alive. I'm glad this isn't Judgment Day."

The doctor looks down at his chalkboard.

MARRIAGE FOUR, he writes.

"Hindus don't have a Day of Judgment, do they?" Noah asks, checking the tape counter.

Rama raps loudly on the chalkboard. He demands Noah's attention. He wants an answer.

"None with four. Natasha lives now in Montreal."

MARRIAGE FIVE?

"Joey. Los Angeles. No, probably New York."

Drawn out on the chalkboard, the chart looks like this:

MARRIAGE	WIFE	CHILDREN	CITY
1	SHELLEY LEVINE		CHICAGO
2	ANNA JONES	JIM & CAROL	BOULDER
3	DOLORES DIVINE	ARIEL	NEW YORK
4	NATASHA KAMINSKY		MONTREAL
5	HOLLY HOLLANDER	JOEY	LOS ANGELES -NEW YORK

The doctor erases the chalkboard.

MARRIAGE ONE. WHO LEFT WHO? he writes.

"Who left *whom*," Noah repeats.

"I left," says Noah, scratching his belly. "I never should have married her in the first place. I was a kid, 18, just out of high school. She lived in an apartment complex a few blocks away from where I lived. We met coming out of a movie theater— *Rebel Without A Cause,* with James Dean and Natalie Wood. You know, after all these years, that film still stands up. Do you go to movies? Oh, yeah, I'm sorry. Anyway, meeting someone so sweet and warm, making friends with someone whom I already felt I knew, whom I seemed always to have known, in a way it was like finding a sister. Can you understand?

"Soon I'd go over to her house to watch *Ozzie and Harriet* and the *Phil Silvers Show.* We watched Dick Clark's *American Bandstand* and tried dancing to four-sided pop music. Dinah Shore, Jo Stafford, Frank Sinatra, Tony Bennett. I know, I know. The names don't mean much to you. It was just before Elvis Presley. Before the Beatles. Before Maharishi's Transcendental Meditation.

"Later, we married and went to the University of Illinois at Navy Pier. In those days, it was called Harvard on the Rocks. Shelley wore black leotards and sexy eye shadow like a raccoon. We had a little apartment and a couple times a week smoked marijuana. We'd get stoned, make a whole bunch of spaghetti, go to roller skating rinks—there was one on Kedzie Avenue—and listen to Teresa Brewer singing *Music! Music! Music!* and skate around in circles. We loved it. Or Kay Starr singing *Wheel of Fortune.* And Shelley looked like Kay Starr. Dark hair cut short, bright red lipstick—when she wasn't being a beatnik—a big smile and dimple on her cheek."

Noah closes his eyes.

"For money, I worked as a cub reporter, and even pitched a couple seasons for the Chicago Blackstones."

Drifting in and out of consciousness, he continues.

"One night as we were making love—Buddy Holly singing *Peggy Sue,* "*pretty pretty pretty,*" her teddy bears bouncing up and down on the creaky bed—Shelley began to cry.

"'Am I hurting you?' I asked.

"'Oh, no,' she said.

"'Is something wrong?' I asked.

"'No, it's alright.

"'But you're crying,' I said.

"'No, no. It's nothing. It's just. Nothing.'

"Later, we made love again."

"'You, you,' she said afterwards.

"I learn slowly,'" he says. "Now, thirty years later, when a woman says, 'You, you' in that way, I know that something wonderful has happened. That 'you, you' is better than any declaration of love. In my experience, a woman may say that once or twice when you first get to know her, and again once or twice during a marriage. I've also known women to say that just before a marriage and then never again.

"Of course that 'you, you' could also be said in an accusatory way, but that's not the way Shelley said it.

"One night Shelley asked me, 'Where do you feel love in your body?'

"'Not in my arms. Not in my feet or legs. Not in my head. I guess I feel it in the middle of my chest,' I said.

"'So do I. That's why most people associate love with the heart, even people who never really thought about it.'

"'What do you love best about me, Noah? Would you like me to tell you first? That you love me, that's what I love best about you. That you love me the way I am, almost the way my mother loved me. You don't try to change anything about me.

"'Whatever people say who want to change you, what they're really saying is, 'You're not good enough the way you are.' Noah, you're like a brother to me, and a lover. I'll tell you something I never told anyone. I love myself so much because deep down I know I have good taste. And your love for me shows me you have good taste,' she joked.

"'I know people who have a lot going for them, but they think anyone who falls for them has bad taste. Like my girlfriend Joanne. Joanne thinks there's something wrong with any man who falls for her. Good guys come along and she complains, "There's something wrong with that guy." Guys who are going to treat her bad, who could care less, that's what she's looking for. She's managed to convince herself that's what she deserves.'

"I've fallen for women like that, beautiful women," Noah sighs. "I went ahead and risked everything for them. I'd go so far as to pretend I didn't care, thinking if I played it cool that would help.

"But I'm not good at hiding what I feel. If I pretend I'm indifferent, women see right through me. If I pretend to be cool, the coolness is like a frame for what I'm really feeling. It makes everything that's churning away inside show up all the more. And I get clobbered by people who really have cool.

"Marriage is something you have to give your whole mind to. I've had trouble doing that."

EXPLAIN TROUBLE.

"I see a woman like Shelley or Anna and long for her. Then if we marry, I end up feeling trapped. And then I feel guilty because I am not happy. I feel angry and cheated because I feel guilty instead of happy. So maybe I'll have an affair. Then I feel guilty about that because when I have affairs it makes it difficult for me to give my whole mind to the marriage.

"So each time I marry I try to cleanse myself."

CLEANSE YOURSELF?

"One thing I did before I married Anna was to fast for forty-eight hours. Fasting before you marry is a custom in our family."

Noah clenches his fists. "Sonofabitch!" He longs to return to his old high school and run, one last time, both arms swinging, into a crowd of his biggest classmates. *Alle yevonim hoben ayn ponim.*"

"At fifteen, what bothered me the most was my mother died without announcement."

WITHOUT ANNOUNCEMENT? Rama writes.

"You know what I mean. A proclamation. A formal statement that my mother was resigning. Maybe I could have talked some sense into her head." Noah pauses. "The warranty ran out," he explains.

YOU HAVE WARRANTY YOUR WIFE WILL STAY WITH YOU?

"It's in my car. It's in the glove compartment of my Volvo."

YOU HAVE WARRANTY IN YOUR GLOVE COMPARTMENT?

"It also says you're supposed to make me feel better."

Rama's eyes crinkle. His mouth opens. He begins to shake. "*Sssst,*" he laughs.

"After my mother died, I thought if I saw her walking down the street I wouldn't recognize her. I found it hard to remember what she looked like. I don't think my Mom ever wanted kids. She wanted to go on stage, she wanted a career. I'm proud of her, my mom, being a beauty queen. But it's not something a kid wants his mother involved in."

A SON LOSES HIS MOTHER. HE LOSES HIMSELF, Rama writes.

"What's that?"

Rama ignores the question. DO FIVE WIVES EQUAL ONE MOTHER?

"You mean like a trade-off or something?" Noah says.

Rama raps on his chalkboard. Noah blinks. "Huh?"

MARRIAGE ONE. REASON FOR LEAVING? Rama writes. He turns and invites Noah to read.

"Reason for leaving?" Noah says into his microphone.

"Did you ever see that Michael Cacoyannis movie *Zorba the Greek*? Anthony Quinn plays Zorba, a zesty old Greek who, in one scene, is feeling trapped and frustrated. Zorba sums up his situation: 'Wife, children, house, everything. The full catastrophe.' Well, that's what I felt with Shelley and, later, with Anna. I began with a craving. I craved sex, companionship, a beautiful home.

"And it wasn't long after we married that I panicked. Suddenly I felt ten years older and twenty pounds heavier. I was immature. I'm sure Shelley and Anna felt trapped and frustrated in their own way. And if they didn't, they had every right to."

Noah writes:

> Oh, my God, what was I thinking? What am I doing here? Still, better an East Indian physician than a therapist prescribing Equanil, Librium, Miltown, Quaaludes, Seconal, Thalidomide, Thorazine, Triavil, Valium. Better this dude than stingy, squeeze of the toothpaste tube fifty-minutes-and-you're-out-of-here therapy."

His father, Noah decided, had something in common with therapists he'd come to know. Like those therapists, the sharp-eyed comic subscribed to the notion that people create their own version of reality.

"You want to know about the world, Noah?" his father once asked. "You think God created the world? A joke. For most people God didn't need to create the world. Such a favor. In their minds they create the world every day. And what a world. Money.

Terrible enemies. A little pleasure. Now and then a scapegoat.

"A big shot philosopher said to me once, 'David, the world is as you see it.'

"And you, you *shmegegge*," his father goes on, "every couple years you create a new world, a new family, new children. Such a blessing you've been. Thank God your mother's not here to see it."

WHAT MADE YOU LEAVE WIFE #1? writes the doctor.

"Not only did I feel trapped, I felt bored. I was bored with myself. So I guess I blamed her. But it wasn't her, it was me. I was too young. I hadn't experienced— Also, by that time I was into playing a certain role, and no one partner was enough for me.

"Is this alright. Maybe I'm boring you. Shall I go on?"

CONTINUE.

"Once my first wife and I agreed to meet at noon by the fountain in the main lobby of the Drake Hotel in Chicago. I got there on time. I looked everywhere, but I couldn't find her. After thirty minutes, I left to run some errands. An hour later I returned. I found her waiting for me behind a pillar. She'd been waiting there since noon. I found her by accident. It never occurred to me Shelley would be waiting behind a pillar with her back to the fountain.

"'Why are you waiting here behind a pillar?' I asked. 'How am I supposed to find you if you're hiding?'

"I mention this because I knew in that moment the marriage was over. At the same time I understood how destructive self-involvement can be. I knew very well she wanted me to hunt for her, really search the lobby, explore the entire hotel, make a fool of myself if I had to. In the months we'd been married, I hadn't done these things on the intimate level one is supposed to do them. I hadn't tenderly searched and explored and gotten to know her. And this was her way of showing me I stood a good chance of losing her. Anyway, that's how it seemed to me.

"Who was it I was married to? I didn't know who Shelley was any more than I knew who I was. I do know what I turned into—a young, sex-hungry journalist, constrained, uncommunicative, heartless and ambitious. Frankly, as a husband I was no bargain. You're nodding, you understand.

"I was afraid of what searching for her would mean. To search as she wanted me to would mean growing up, coming out of myself. I know that's a cliché, and I'm sorry. After a few months with Shelley I thought, 'I'm not giving her—and am probably incapable of giving—what she needs. At that point there was no woman I could have spent the rest of my life with.'

"Poor Shelley, the beautiful girl from West Rogers Park. I see her now in her white cotton, high necked, no-sex-before-marriage Victorian nightgown with the hundreds of little rosebuds. I want to say, 'How clean and fresh and virginal you were and, in some essential way, I believe you are so still, to this day. Yes, I love you wife number one and I'm sorry I was such a schmuck.'

"We still write and talk to one another on the phone. We're what people call 'best friends.' Once I sent her a story I wrote that touched on the marriage. She wrote back saying, 'I found your story great fun to read. It didn't tax my sense of humor at all, only my willing suspension of disbelief.' Hmm. I wonder what she meant by that."

Rama scarcely blinks. He's listening, but turns and, so it seems to Noah, glances longingly at the TV.

11

Marriage #2
In Praise of Justices of the Peace

9:00 A.M.

MARRIAGE TWO. WHO LEFT WHO? Rama writes.

"Marriage two. Who left *whom*?" Noah repeats.

"She left," he answers.

WHY? Rama writes, and heads to the kitchen to brew some chai.

"I was unfaithful," Noah says, raising his voice. He's feeling more ashamed than ever. He's feeling guilt just as he felt guilt when he was sleeping around. He thinks of the times with nurse Henrietta Van Buren under the stars in Ithaca, New York's Sapsucker Woods. He recalls how once she kneeled beside him in an oak-lined, book-filled study. Dr. Van Buren taught a graduate seminar in Eighteenth Century English Literature. Jonathan Swift. Samuel Johnson. Alexander Pope.

"I am his Highness' dog at Kew. Pray tell me, Madam, whose dog are you?" he'd whispered in her ear.

"Remember, every dog is entitled to one bite," she'd said.

"Maybe I deserved it," Noah says, opening his briefcase. "Maybe I got what I deserved," he goes on, putting a fresh tape in the machine. "Sometimes it's comforting to get what you deserve," he smiles, following the doctor into the kitchen. "It shows there's a logic to our lives. Things don't happen for no reason, there's a law of cause and effect."

When the water boils, Rama stirs in six teaspoons of black tea. He covers the pot and lets it simmer.

CHAI, he writes on the chalkboard.

A few minutes later, he turns off the heat and strains the tea. Next he adds honey, samples the brew and adds more sweetener. Then he heats a pot of milk, pours it cup by cup into the tea and stirs in fresh ground cardamom, cinnamon, cloves, and nutmeg. Again he samples the brew. Smacking his lips in approval, reaching for a strainer, he fills two white mugs with a liquid the color of creamy cocoa.

"Whew! That's delicious," Noah says, renewed.

Returning to his seat in front of the TV, Rama brings the cup to his lips and invites Noah to continue.

"Yes, Anna finally left," he says, checking the tape counter. "Neither she nor I had really wanted to get married. At a time when there weren't other alternatives, at a time when it was the right thing to do, Anna and I were propelled into marriage by an unexpected pregnancy. Do I sound defensive? Do I sound like a talking head? I am defensive. I am a talking head, okay? Hell, doctor, neither of us liked the idea of having to get married. But we did and she did make the best of it. She was a fine mother and she loved to entertain. Because of her I advanced in my career. She created a terrific home. In fact, I didn't realize how important home was until the marriage ended. That was one thing I learned from the marriage: that I sincerely wanted a home, family, and children. I learned too that I tended to impose a script on women and limited their growth."

A SCRIPT? writes the doctor.

"A text for an ideal marriage. I wanted a devoted wife and muse, a nurturer and a general factotum all in one person. I had a play already written for what I felt would be the perfect partner.

"Then when I had what I wanted, and I had it with Anna,

I didn't want it. I wanted what I wanted within the marriage, but at the same time I wanted what I wanted outside the marriage. I wanted Henrietta Van Buren (love among the first editions). I wanted a student named Debbie Trillium (Debbie with her torn lace undergarments). I wanted Yolanda Yasmin ("darlink, we're animals first and human second."). I was a world class jerk, Rama, and probably still am! All the time I was hungry for more. Emily Dickinson writes, Is there not a *sweet wolf in us that wants what it wants?* I wanted Anna's stability but for some reason that wasn't enough. I wanted that and more. As much as I wanted to stay with her, I refused to compromise. I was thinking feature story, feature story, feature story. That wasn't so bad. But I was also pant pant panting around. I'd ask myself, what else is out there? What am I missing? I had the idea that adventure, particularly adventures with other women, lots of other women, would help me become a better writer.

"So I left wife #1, and wife #2 left me."

YOU PRACTICED THE YOGA OF SELF-DECEPTION. VERY POPULAR YOGA. WHAT DID YOU LEARN FROM THIS PRACTICE? Rama writes.

"What did I learn? I learned that when I lied to Shelley or to Anna, I made my spouses into the enemy. When I deceived Shelley or Anna, when I misled them, caused them to believe first one lie, then another, I did what warriors are trained to do: deceive your enemy. Immobilize your enemy so you can do what you want to them. I learned that lies, like it or not, are merciless. Lies kill. Lies kill the family. Lies kill spouses. Lies, at the very least, kill something in one's spouse. They wound children. I learned that lies are irrevocable. Once I had an affair and lied, I found there was no way to go back and make things right again. I learned these things, but of course that didn't stop me from going on having affairs and telling lies."

SEX IS AN ADDICTION, writes the doctor. Erasing that, he writes,

Noah wants a teaspoon of crushed aspirin. A six-pack of cold beer. An antidote to the end of love. If he could, he'd gobble them all down at the same time. He's out of control. My God, he thinks, I'm losing it.

He stands up to leave.

The doctor hasn't finished with him yet. Again, he raps loudly on the little board.

Noah, in a rush of remembering, sees Anna:

"Petite. Five foot two. A professional dancer with very tiny, very delicate hands and feet. She had jet black hair, dark brown eyes and had studied ballet, but also Indian and Indonesian dance. We met at a reception after one of her performances. She was nineteen and had never been with a man before. For the second or third time in my life, I began writing poetry. I courted her with amateurish rhyming poems. I'll be honest. It excited me to introduce her to what I knew about sex. But as a dancer, as a woman discovering her *shakti,* as she called it, her power, I think she knew more than I did.

"Anyway, when Anna became pregnant, we eloped and got married in Cross Lake, Illinois.

"I remember Jenny, the Justice of the Peace, hugging us both after the ceremony. We were with her for about an hour, but in that time she became our family. I remember her telling us that she and her husband had once been Wisconsin dairy farmers. "Like Ma and Pa Kettle," she laughed. I still remember the woman's cinnamon butter smile and those old-fashioned granny glasses. And how she squinted to read the words inside our gold wedding bands: *Forget Me Not.*

"Anna's parents were well-to-do Episcopalian lawyers from Coldwell & Hawkhover, a law firm in Evanston. They hated to see their daughter marry what they called 'that Jew Professor.'

Anna was three months pregnant and a traditional Church wedding just wasn't in the cards. The Justice of the Peace filled in for our families. It was she, Jenny, who gave the bride away, and that moved me. Do you understand?

"'You're beautiful, Anna,' she said before we left. I felt she was blessing Anna, and I was proud of my bride. Then Jenny looked me over and again nodded. Somehow I felt I passed her inspection.

"'So many couples come here to be married. When I see cold fish eyes, sometimes I wonder. What's out there for people like that? Whatever becomes of them? But then what becomes of any of us?' she said."

"I'd call the marriage a success. It dried up in the end when I began sleeping around, but we had some good years together and, thank God, Jim and Carol turned out all right."

WIFE TWO LEFT, Rama P. Rama writes.

"I believe if I really tried I could have kept that one together. Yes, Anna left. She went off and married her fifty-eight-year-old therapist and, at the same time, it was all over with Henrietta Van Buren, the other woman. Jim, my son, went with Anna and I lived alone with my daughter, Carol, for about three months. Then I met my third wife, Dolores Divine, an interior designer from New York. Shelley says I practiced on Anna, got confidence from being with her, got attractive, she says, whatever that means, in ways I wasn't before. And I got into a relationship I wouldn't have been in if I hadn't first been married to Anna. Suddenly I was in the position of having to care for a woman I loved but who, it turned out, was a whole lot needier than I was."

12

Marriage #3
The Sexual Revolution

10:00 A.M.

Noah pauses, pours tea for the doctor and himself, presses Record-Play, and the interview continues.

MARRIAGE THREE. WHO LEFT WHOM? YOU OR DOLORES?

"When I found out what was going on I threw her out," he says, revved up, hardly conscious of what he's saying. "She was unfaithful," he roars. "She gave me a taste of my own medicine. She slept with the newspaper boy, the census taker, the furnace repair man, the furnace, the hot water tank, the front fence, the back fence, the lawn mower, the pile of leaves in the front yard, the wild flowers by the side of the house...

"Doctor, I didn't think I could live through another break up. I was ready to do just about anything to stay with Dolores. For one thing I was terrified of losing Ariel, my daughter. I had bonded with Ariel more than my other children—maybe because I was right there in the delivery room when she was born.

"But Dolores. Dolores wanted to sleep with three or four people at a time. In the 1960s and '70s people smoked pot and did things like that. I said, 'No wife-swapping, no swinging. Think about Ariel. You're a Mommy, remember? And I'm a Daddy.'

"Her pulling away, or wanting to pull away, hurt. Never mind three or four people: I began to see that just Dolores and me alone was too much. It took a while, but I finally came to my senses.

"You know what her last words were? 'I'll see you in the next world.' And when she saw the expression on my face, she said, 'I'm not angry with you. At least I said I wanted to see you in the next world.'"

"Ariel, about two or three years old at the time, stayed with me. I raised her. 'You'll do better looking after her than I will,' Dolores said. 'You can have custody.' What a relief that was. There was no court fight. No custody battle.

"Dolores has been married three times so far and has had three daughters with three different men and each of the men, myself included, raised the daughter he fathered."

THIS WAS A MARRIAGE? writes Rama.

"For the first couple years we were faithful, or at least I was. Then all hell broke loose.

"From the day we met—on a beach in Santa Monica—it was a combination of thunder, lightning, and intercity rivalry: her New York The Big Apple First City Master Race versus my pip squeak bourgeois Second City Chicago. In her view, people who grew up in Manhattan and attended Music and Art High School are privileged human beings, wiser, tougher and more deserving than anyone else. So yes, there was some tension.

"'Where I come from, we make our own rules and don't have to be touched by anything,' she said.

"'And if you leave a mess, who cleans up?' I said.

"'My father's a surgeon. There's always someone to clean up.'

"Actually, her father was a proctologist."

HOW DID YOU TWO MEET? the doctor writes.

"I was between wives and house-sitting for friends in Los Angeles. I shouldn't have been snooping, but one evening I looked in their closet and found a stack of magazines: *Playboy* and *Kama Sutra*. Stuff like that gets imprinted on your brain. It's a trap. Anyway, I remember reading the caption under one of the photos:

5'2", eyes of blue, 34, 24, 34, Dolores ('Beverly
Blueeyes') Divine is studying Interior Design at
State University of New York (SUNY).

"I confess it. I desired her. But what could I offer such a woman?

"My mother used to say, 'Be careful what you wish for because you'll get it.'

"You know that phrase 'Talk about coincidence'? A couple
weeks later I was jogging on a beach in Santa Monica. A woman
in a Day-Glo bikini caught my eye, but at first I didn't recognize
her. I stopped to say hello to the guy she was with, a screenwriter.
Someone I knew. He introduced me. 'This is my ex-wife Dolores
Divine.' He was courting Dolores, trying to win her back for the
second or third time. Then it dawned on me: Beverly Blueeyes,
the *Kama Sutra* centerfold."

KAMA SUTRA?

"*Kama Sutra* in this country is a slick psychedelic art magazine."

Seeing the look of puzzlement on the doctor's face, Noah
adds, "It's published in New York and it has lots of interviews
with stars and photographs of people making love and the
latest fashions.

"As it turned out, Dolores was an interior designer for the
stars, some big names. She liked mingling with those people. It
was great while it lasted—about a year—and she made lots of
money. Then they turned to someone else. Anyway, I said the first
thing that came into my mind. 'You look familiar. Haven't we
met before?'

"Her ex saw I was interested and was ready to take a swing at me."

Pressing Eject, Noah removes tape #3, labels it *Dec. 23,
Mt. Chakra* and puts in another.

"Doctor, I'm boring you. When you've had enough..."

Rama gestures with his hand. NO, NO...CONTINUE.

"Holly says I'm a woman-pleaser, that I'll stop at nothing.

She says women can tell this about a man right off the bat. The truth is Dolores was gorgeous. Outrageous. I even liked her big mouth, *nautch* girl sassiness. I couldn't hide what I was feeling and went all-out to land her. It's embarrassing to say, but looking back on that courtship, I'd say Dolores landed me.

"Doctor, what's your position on beauty? What do you know about beauty? What is beauty?"

IT IS A PART OF DESIRE WHICH ADMIRES THE OBJECT. IT IS PART OF THE DESIRE AND NOT THE OBJECT.

"Is that a roundabout way of saying Beauty is in the eye of the beholder? You're putting emphasis on desire, but you're still saying the same thing aren't you?"

FEAR AND ANGER AND DESIRE WORK TOGETHER. WHERE THERE IS DE-SIRE, THERE IS FEAR AND ANGER.

FLASHBACK:

Mountain View University, Vancouver, British Columbia
SEPTEMBER

Dolores was blissfully pregnant even before they married. One year after Ariel's birth, Noah got a job teaching at Mountain View University. Before leaving for Canada, he dreamt of pine trees and an airplane which, lacking flight crew and engines, was made largely of wood. With a window seat on the starboard side of the plane, he prepared to disembark when he saw that the cabin area had no other covering than fragrant greenery, the fresh-cut branches of evergreens. But already the plane was taxiing out of a hangar into a clearing in a dense forest. Picking up speed, it raced across a frozen lake. At last, airborne, a hundred or more feet above the ground, all he could see in the craft's wake was ice and snow.

On Labor Day, he and his wife were invited to a Beginning-of-the-Term Faculty Function. Dolores dressed up for the occasion: black linen jacket and a white silk jumpsuit. Dolores, however, made a point of smoking hashish beforehand.

"If they meet me when I'm stoned, Noah, they won't think I'm weird or something when they meet me again and I'm still stoned. Do you know what I mean? I can't believe the academic mind. And Canadian academics are the worst. Did you meet that Welsh professor from McGill? Or the dork from Saskatchewan? They're so narrow-minded. And here I am a faculty wife at, at— what's this place called? The University of Downsview, right?"

"Mountain View University."

"Alright, alright. It could be the University of the Moon for all I care. Oh, Noah. And I'll have to socialize with other faculty wives. I'll just smoke a couple times a day. I expect I'll be stoned the entire time we're here."

"Dolores, we could be here for two years. Maybe more."

"So? Might as well start now," she said, reaching for her water pipe.

"Well, what do you think of Vancouver?" asked the head of the University's Communications Department, a jowly, steak-and-kidney-pie academic. "All I know is it blows my mind to see gardens in front of so many peoples' houses," Noah said as Professor Alistair McGlashan refilled his goblet with Bristol Cream sherry. "And I like looking out on English Bay. We like the West End."

"Well, we're glad to give you a little respite. America sounds in a bad way right now. I don't mind saying our Department is pleased to have been able to lure you away from the States.

"Oh, by the way, Noah, were you ever in the Service?"

"I was in the Air Force for three years."

"Well, at least you're not a draft dodger."

"Draft dodger? No, but I am opposed to what they're doing in the war. Nixon, Johnson...The whole bunch of them. You've seen my work. I've said as much in print. But I'm here to teach Journalism."

"Well, I trust you won't be too vocal about your views?"

"My views?" Fuck you, he thought. I'll teach and, if it comes up, I'll speak my mind.

"Noah, we're a new university. We've come in for some scrutiny by our critics."

"You mean the government? The Canadian government?"

"Yes, and the Province. We need to be—how should I put it?—circumspect. We can't condone anti-war demonstrations. Or drugs. Our critics are alarmed by the influx of radicals. Now, while we're pleased to have you here as our guest, I have to ask that you, hmm, hmm, respect our customs."

'How do you stand it here?' he longed to say. 'How am I going to stand it?' Noah sucked in his lips. 'I'm a guest, I'm a guest,' he reminded himself.

"You know I'll teach just as I was contracted to do," he said, "but I don't know about this 'influx of radical' business."

Radical, he thought. Ultra, revolutionary, subversive, Bolshevik, anarchist, nihilist, collectivist, utopian...

Radicalis, the word means 'getting at the roots of things.'

Say he's fired and called upon to defend himself.

'How was I to draw the line between respecting your customs and working and living a life which led to the resumé and features which made you hire me in the first place?' he'll say. 'Was I expected to become someone other than who it was you interviewed and hired?'

For now he'll keep his mouth shut.

"By the way, Alistair, you know what brought me to Canada. What brought you here?"

"My family moved here from New England. We left because of the Revolution," said McGlashan.

"What do you mean, Revolution?" he asked.

"The American Revolution. My ancestors left Massachusetts after the Boston Tea Party. We're United Empire Loyalists," McGlashan said, throwing back his shoulders.

"Alistair, you mean your family's been here for over 200 years? That's incredible."

Newmark scratched his head. Dolores is going to fall over laughing, he thought. 'Honey, I have to tell you something. These people think Paul Revere is the enemy.'

A couple years earlier Noah had written, "Silver Screen College? what am I doing at Silver Screen College?" Now the question was, "Canada, what am I doing in Canada?"

Turning to the hors d'oeuvre table, he watched Dolores sipping champagne and scooping up goose liver pate. Dolores was surrounded by four academics, men she later identified as "Tweedledum and Tweedledee from the University of Somewhere or Other," "Professor I-Have-A-Degree-From-Somewhere-Better-Than-MountainView," and "Professor Unhireable-Anywhere-But-Here." He arrived to see Dolores whirl around and giggle, "Oh, Mrs. McGlashan, you're funny. What do I like to read? Well, I like cookbooks, I like those envelopes filled with coupons, and the *TV Guide*."

"You must be a wonderful cook, my dear," said Mrs. McGlashan, seemingly charmed by Dolores.

"Not really, Mrs. McGlashan. I just like reading about food. I hate shopping, don't you? And washing dishes afterwards. Ugh."

"What about TV? What are your favorite shows?" asked the man she called Unhireable-Anywhere-But-Here.

"Oh, we don't own a TV Professor. I just like knowing what's on and reading about re-runs and movies and things, don't you?"

"Umm, I understand you've done some modeling," remarked I-Have-A-Degree.

"You must be thinking about my being in *Kama Sutra*. Actually, I'm an interior designer—and a muralist. You'll have to see the new one I started. Wait'll the owners come back from France. Actually, I think they'll like it."

"Hmm. Did you ever visit the *Playboy* mansion?"

"A long time ago. I used to work out in Hugh Hefner's gym—an underground gym—every day. He has, I think it's called an aviary. That's a funny word. A-vi-ary. Anyway, he has his own birds and bees. And a big fizzy Jacuzzi filled with gin.

"Of course *Kama Sutra's* a different magazine...

"Oh, hi, Noah. Gee, honey, why the big smile? Do you have something funny to tell me? Who's this?"

"Alistair McGlashan is head of the Communications Department. He's my boss. Alistair, I'd like you to meet my wife, Anna Jones. Anna, dear, meet Alistair McGlashan. He's..."

"Anna Jones?" Dolores wailed. "No." Clenching her fists, she sobbed, "I'm number *three*, Noah, remember?" Then, pounding *left, right, left, right* on her husband's chest, she clarified for him and, at the same time, explained to McGlashan and his bug-eyed wife and the others, the cause of her action, "Anna was your second wife.

Anna...*punch*....was...*punch*....his...*punch*....second wife."

Hearing Noah cough and then shake, he feared she'd injured him, feared he might respond in kind. Instead, she saw him double over and rock from side to side cackling. Inspired by Noah's example, Dolores herself began to laugh.

Mountain View University

JANUARY

Four months after the party, Dolores and Noah surveyed their backyard for the tallest, healthiest, most vicious-looking weeds they could find, ugly, rank giants brimming with vim and vigor. These they spent two rainy afternoons digging out by the roots figuring where dozens of healthy weeds thrived, dozens of marijuana plants would thrive as well. Of course they waited until the moon was in Scorpio, the most auspicious time for planting marijuana.

Later, under the cover of darkness, after disposing of the native weeds, he with a pitchfork and shovel, she with a rake and hoe, made a fresh assault on the thirty-by-thirty foot garden. Their bodies tingling, their voices low, dripping sweat and rain, they poured the requisite fish fertilizer. Then, raising their muddy knees, dancing in circles, they planted seedlings imported from Mexico.

"See," Dolores said later that night, as they planted rows of corn to camouflage the marijuana, "You don't think I have a spiritual side, but I do."

"I saw you out here last night in the tent. I didn't say anything because I thought you were meditating."

"That's right," Dolores nodded, rake in hand, "I'm a pantheist. By the way, I like that new tent."

"Good. It was on sale. But...pantheist? What do you know about pantheism?"

"Come on! Give me credit for something, Noah. It means God is nature, and I tend to like nature a lot. I get my spirit from that."

Shading her hash pipe with a rain hat, she took a another toke.

"Noah, why do you think people want to repeat traumatic

things?" she asked.

I don't know. Why do you think?"

"To see if they can make it turn out differently."

"Who is God anyway?" she asked.

"They say God is the Unmoved Mover," replied her mate on his hands and knees in the marijuana swamp.

"Isn't God to do anymore with love? That doesn't sound so loving and affectionate."

"What would you prefer, Dolores?"

"That God would be the Moved Unmover."

"You're saying you'd like God to be more involved in your life?"

"Yes. Emotionally involved."

"Well, Dee, you are special. Who else would ask God for a sweetheart deal?"

❖❖❖

"Hey, Dolores, I have a new poem for you."

"Say it to me."

Resting on his shovel, Noah declaimed:

Stars falling,
lovers
flying
the band playing,
drunks at their shorthand,
the moon at its easel,
dogs listening
without objection—
the world
waltzes
into space.

"Is that it?"

"Yeah. Maybe I'll start a book called *Lotus Land*."

"But that poem doesn't rhyme."

"Yeah. Mmm. You don't like it. I can tell."

"Like? What's there to like? Oh, Noah. I have a question. I don't understand about the shorthand."

"What don't you understand?"

"I don't understand what it means."

Every second night they watered and weeded. When the temperature dropped, they brought out smudge pots to protect the greenery from frost. On her sewing machine, Dolores made tall, clear plastic cones, "marijuana rain jackets" she called them, to safeguard the exotic weeds. Some balmy evenings they slept in the tent with Ariel to be near their darlings.

"Daddy, book..." Ariel would say as he prepared her evening bottle.

Other times, stubborn, unwilling to do something, Ariel joked about his name. "No, no, Noah...." she'd laugh.

Whenever Ariel cried for a bottle, or to be changed, it was Noah she asked for. "Daddy, daddy..."

Those evenings when it didn't rain, he'd place her on his shoulders and, with or without Dolores, walk through Stanley Park to Prospect Point and back. Best of all about the walks was the swelling in his chest and the sensation of Ariel's breath in his ears.

So it was that Noah became his daughter's caregiver, Noah Mother-man, the spouse who yearned for stability. Dolores, for her part, pulled in another direction.

MARCH

"Don't you find sleeping out under the stars an aphrodisiac?" Dolores asked, opening the tent flap, watching the moon-struck marijuana grow.

"What don't you find an aphrodisiac?" he laughed, pouring Dolores' favorite drink, pink champagne on the rocks. Stirring this refresher with a swizzle stick, Dolores waited for the fizz to leave the wine. Only then would she wiggle out of her earth-smudged jeans and lace undergarments. And only then would she drink.

"Nothing turns me on to the company of women more than women. Being with you makes me want to be with you," he said snuggling close.

"Yeah, I see," said Dolores, reaching for a joint. "And what turns you on to marriage is being married."

"I'm a romantic! Mmm, baby, that feels good."

"Noah, tell me something. Why do you marry? I mean, what does marriage allow, what does it do for you?"

"I don't understand."

"What do you get from marriage that you couldn't get in some other way? Without the benefit of the pledge?"

"Dolores, how well you phrase that! I like the way your mind works when you're stoned."

"Stop joking. Noah, I'm your wife—your third wife, remember?—and I wanna know."

"Okay. The way I see it, people who don't marry are hedging their bets. I may be crazy, but I've never been one to hedge my bets. I'm one of those all or nothing people."

"And how many people are you prepared to marry?"

"You're the one I want to stay with, Dolores. But if it comes to that, I'd probably marry again."

"Why? What does marriage do for you?"

"We all need some doing, don't we?" Noah said, playing on

the word "do."

"Be serious, Noah."

"I am being serious. When I marry, I somehow feel I'm doing my duty. And if I'm done in by the marriage that I've done something wrong, that it's my own fault."

"You make it sound like voting."

"That's what I was brought up to believe. That whatever it is I need, whatever that doing is, I've somehow convinced myself, or I've been convinced, that marriage does it for me. That I have to be out there every four years or so like a good citizen."

"You're playing with words. What a definition of citizenship! You sound like my high school English teacher, Mrs. Burns."

"Was I playing with words when I said 'I do' when we got married?

"How would I know if you were playing with words? Were you?"

"Of course not. I made a vow. I meant what I said. 'I do. I do.' And in case you've forgotten, Dolores, I have lived on my own."

"Huh? What does that mean?"

"What that means is I haven't merely gone from woman to woman without thinking what I'm getting into."

"You're one in a million, Noah."

"Am I supposed to take that as a compliment? It somehow doesn't sound like a compliment."

"You're addicted to marriage the way gamblers are to gambling."

"You know me, Dolores. As I told you, I don't do anything half-hearted."

"That's your problem, bub."

APRIL

"Noah, let's smoke some of that new hash," she said one night before they went out to work in the garden. "Where did I put those matches? And where's that cassette player? Mmm, that's good stuff."

"It's from Morocco. You can tell by the smell. Here. See? It smells like an old baseball mitt. And rosin. Talk to your hairdresser, Dee. See if you can score for more. What's his name?"

"Mario"

"Yeah, Mario. See if you can score another ten grams. It's funny. Before we met I only used to smoke once or twice a month. Now I'm a lotus eater and my mind's begun to curdle."

"Why do you smoke with me, Noah?"

"I do it because it's part of how we make out. I do it to keep up with you. You know, you smoke the way a 12-year-old might devour a Baby Ruth bar or a box of Cracker Jack. There's something All-American about the way you do dope."

"All-American?" says Dolores, taking offense. "What does that mean?"

"It means you're wholesome. You still have this 1960s cheerleader look about you: blonde hair, blue eyes, rosy cheeks, nothing sinister or weird. And your eyes never get red when you smoke. You're childlike, if you know what I mean, an innocent of sorts."

"Come off it."

"All I'm saying is your love of dope hasn't messed you up—completely—and if it turns out you're addicted to weed, well, I'm addicted to being with you. Anyway, I'm not sure you'd be with me if I didn't smoke. You need someone to share that with you.

"Dolores, did you ever hear of Circe? Circe, the sorceress?"

"Shirley? Shirley who? The what?"

Noah woke an hour later to the sound of fog horns and the scent of burning matches. Seeing him open his eyes, Dolores switched on her portable cassette player and, hesitating for a moment, sang along in the moonlight with Bob Dylan, *Lay, Lady, Lay*.

His back and legs sore from hours of kneeling, stretching and tugging weeds, the gentleman pot farmer stretched out on the air mattress and once more shut his eyes. He went back to dreaming of rototilling the back yard with a heavy vibrating machine. His partner in this operation turned out to be a blonde, blue-eyed Manhattan farm girl. This New Yorker, this partner in crime, had sweat slippery breasts flecked with pine needles that swayed up and back as she worked by his side. Barefoot, ankle deep in the soft, fresh-smelling earth, she smelled of marijuana, cinnamon, and work.

Awake, determined to keep him awake, Dolores poked her husband with her elbow. "Hey, sleepyhead!" she called as she blew in his ear, "Are you there? Ah, that's better. How did you sleep? Can I touch you?

"I've been thinking," she mused, sitting astride him. "Maybe I'm idealistic, but I believe affairs are opportunities to keep a marriage fresh. And I know I can trust you. I know you love me and that you wouldn't run off with someone else. Would you?"

"Huh? What? What are you talking about?"

"Affairs. If you were to have an affair, you wouldn't leave me, would you?" she said, raising and lowering her hips.

"No," he said, blinking in the darkness, "I wouldn't. But then again, I don't even want to be with another woman."

"Yes, you do. I know you do. And women want their freedom too."

"Sssh. Keep your voice down, Dolores. You'll wake Ariel! You amaze me. You know that? Is it such a sin to want to be faithful?"

"Oh, Noah, you're getting stodgy. You're no fun anymore," she said as he reluctantly withdrew.

Her back to him, suddenly silent, she began to sob.

Noah reached for her hand. "For once in my life I want to be in a close, loving, monogamous relationship, and the woman I'm married to wants me to sleep around."

"It's alright, baby. If you were to have an affair and grow as a result, that would enrich the other woman and me."

"'Enrich the other woman? 'What kind of talk is that?"

"I've been reading this article in *Cosmopolitan*, okay? I really don't think I'd mind. In fact, I'd be glad for it. All I'd ask is that you be honest with me. No lies. I know I don't own you and you don't own me."

"I've done all that, Dolores, okay? Besides, I've got my hands full just satisfying you."

"Look, a woman can have a steak dinner and still want apple pie for dessert. Don't turn into our parents."

His mouth went dry. "Is there something you want to tell me about our sex life?"

"Only what Dr. Gross says: 'Whatever enriches your primary partner, enriches you.' He says that includes your lover or spouse being with another person."

"So that's it. And who does he get to be with? Dr. Jerry Gross. He looks gross. His idea of therapy is gross. He's a Permission Giver. 'Go for the sex. Go for the money. That's the way to succeed. On your mark. Get set. Go. Go for it all, Dolores, and screw anyone who gets in the way.'

"You give him sixty dollars an hour and he'll give you permission to do anything that comes into your head. Or his head, for that matter. It's the Grab, Take, and Screw school of therapy. *Enrich* the other woman! The only thing more swollen about Jerry Gross than his dick is his wallet. He's one of those shrinks who does therapy with an ornament. What's that German word? It means jewelry. *Schmuck*! That's it."

"He doesn't use an ornament."

"What do you mean, 'He doesn't use an ornament'? How the hell would you know?"

"Oh, Noah, come on. I don't sleep with my therapist," she says, opening the tent flap.

"Okay, forget it. Let's forget that gross *macher* and talk about something useful. I've been reading about fertilizer and I have an idea. Let's build a compost heap."

"How do you do that?" Dolores giggled. Off the hook about Gross, she furrowed her brow, eager to learn all she could about marijuana nutrients.

"You begin with a layer of rotted leaves. Then a layer of dirt. Then lime. Caustic lime. Then all our self-help books. Fruit and vegetable peelings. Then a layer of talk about open marriage. Finally you cover the whole thing with plastic sheeting to keep the flies off.

"Here, help me with the sleeping bag. A spider just walked over me."

Again, turning away, Dolores wept. Silvery teardrops, the hot tears of a wronged child, tears shaped like teaspoons, fine flat-ware, flowed out of her eyes. "You're so cruel. I hate you. I can't believe it. You want to do everything your way."

Noah went to her and poured the last of the champagne into her glass. He held the goblet to her lips.

Seizing the moment, Dolores attacked.

"You can put him down if you like, but I've learned from seeing Dr. Gross. There are selfish people—jealous for no reason—and there are people prepared to share their spouses. Liberated people."

"Oh, God, here we go again."

"We're free to come and go and do as we like. We don't have to regard our marriage, or anyone else's, as a life sentence. Why should we have to feel trapped? Only materialists regard their spouses as possessions."

"Dolores, sweetie, speak for yourself. I don't feel trapped. And, speaking of materialists, we both know people who would be more likely to lend you their spouses for the night than the keys to their Mercedes."

"Noah, you're talking about bozo materialistic men. Jerry Gross says non-possessive love is good."

"You can tell him for me his ideas about sex come off bumper stickers. Sshhh, I think Ariel is waking up."

"Tell him yourself. Haven't you ever loved a person without feeling you had to possess her?"

"What about Ariel? We have a kid, Dolores. Let's give her a family. Let's put her first," he said.

"Let me say something…"

"Honey, you're nagging. Dolores Divine, the only woman in this hemisphere who positively nags her husband to have an affair."

"The impulse to be with another person doesn't have to be selfish, does it?"

"Damn you, Dolores, don't you see, what you're asking for is a form of consumerism. Aren't you one of those people who condemns consumerism? But here you are buying into it. Disposable sex. Disposable partners. Disposable marriages. Say I take you up on this open marriage bullshit. I mean, sooner or later you'll find someone who strikes you as better suited to you than me. Or vice versa. Eventually one of us is going to want to trade up, from spouse X to spouse Y."

"Dolores, I'm having to ask myself a question."

"What's the question?"

"Is the fucking I'm getting worth the fucking I'm getting?"

Seeing her wince, Noah sighed. "Poor Angel. You want to

experience everything you can, don't you?"

A flash of lightning. Spats of rain beat on the windows.

Noah blinks. "Sorry about that, doctor," he says, turning to fidget with the tape machine. "Normally, I'm...I'm not a space cadet."

Chalkboard at the ready, the doctor listens.

DIVORCE: SINGLE EVENT FOLLOWED BY SELF-SUSTAINING NUCLEAR REACTION, he writes.

Setting down his teacup, Noah reads Rama's words into the tape machine, presses Rewind, and plays them back.

"Still working," he says, and pops in a new cassette.

"Doctor, after two marriages, I didn't want an open marriage. I had come to really love Dolores and had learned my lesson. I don't think I had really loved her to begin with.

Feverish, Noah recalls the fragrance of Dolores' Shalimar, that tropical scent, the odor of her body after sex and a sauna bath and more sex to come, steam rising from that moist most delectably edible of volcanoes, O Dolores Divine, O creamy and delicious, V for Victory, V for Venus, V for Mt. Venus.

In his heart he addresses Dolores, AKA Beverly Blueeyes:

> O Dolores, how I scaled your heights—and you rode mine to your pleasure—yes, yes, Dolores, those many times ripped on high grade hashish or marijuana or acid, nothing was too good for us, Parsley, Sage, Rosemary and Thyme, O Dolores, yes, let's do it before I write this feature, let's do it after I write this feature, let's do it as I plan to write the feature, let's do it out on Bob Dylan *Highway Sixty-One*, O *Magical Mystery Tour*, O *Sergeant Pepper*, I know you thought and

think to this day that men are fools, O what a
fool I was, O how I gave all for love, Dolores
Dolores, I want you to know I loved your sweet
moist Ever Ready scrumptious rubyfruit nookie
and think well and often of it to this day. I just
didn't want to share you. Or your delights."

Recovering, Noah stammers. "I'm s-sorry," he says. Again, he
begins addressing Rama who, right forearm resting on his head,
closes his eyes as if in meditation. Unperturbed, the doctor seems
not so much to hear as to witness what the writer is saying. Of
course the doctor's heard it all before. Most of the healer's "cases," as
Noah discovered in his interviews, are people like himself.

"At first Dolores was obsessed with being faithful. She seemed
to have the idea that if we had sex each time before I went out
the door—to the post office, to the library—that I'd be true to
her. Well, she was right. For three years I was faithful. It was good.
I mean, I thought it was good. Maybe three years of monogamy
was all Dolores could stand. Then it became boring for her. She
decided she wanted a change. She said, 'You're restricting me.
You're possessive and jealous. I want to be a gypsy. I want my
freedom. When I vacuum the carpet, I want to be able to do it
without wearing clothes. If someone comes to the door, why
should I have to get dressed?

"'My first husband hated it when I went out without wearing my underpants. You don't mind, do you?'

"'I do mind. I mind a lot,' I said. Maybe your ex-husband thought
you were somehow asking his permission for something else. If he
said okay, you'd assume you had his permission to screw around.'

"'I didn't need his permission to screw around. I screwed
around anyway, and I want to keep screwing around."

"When she said that, my heart sank.

"'What kind of person am I with? Who are you? Dolores,

you want an open marriage. I want a subscription to the *Saturday Evening Post*,' I said. "In fact, I'm not so sure I want to be with you."

"What do you want?" she asked. "After two marriages, how can you trust yourself to know what you want? I know it didn't work in my last marriage—having affairs. This time I want to try it a new way. I want you to know when I'm with another man."

MAY

Dolores grabbed her acrylic paints and, barefoot, donning her paisley-patterned, sorceress nightgown, a gift from Noah, began re-working the mural on the wall opposite their bed. Soon figures emerged, three satyrs pursuing three nymphets, three nymphets pursuing three satyrs. Until the marriage ended, Noah would fall asleep and wake to this rendition of his wife's imaginings, scenes of tasteful, rampant lust. Dolores never entirely finished the mural. Night by night, week by week, old satyrs disappeared and were replaced by new. For Noah, it was as if images rose from the bed itself, from their sweaty moaning shouting bouts of hashish-fueled abandon, and attached themselves to the wall.

"Well, Doctor...I knew marriage three was over when we visited my father and my stepmother in Skokie...it's near Chicago. After dinner we talked and watched TV for a while. Around midnight Dolores and I went downstairs to the basement. Our daughter Ariel was already asleep. The room was all fixed up with panel walls and a raised wooden floor, but Dolores said it was damp and had a boggy smell. There was an old bed, a lumpy, hard sofa, actually, that opened up and became a bed. Two people could sleep on it. Dolores had grown up with lots and lots of money.

That night she really understood that I came from an average, middle-class family. Anyone else would think the place was okay, but in Dolores' eyes it was hopeless and if my folks lived in an ugly place well, that meant I was ugly too, tarnished by what I came from. She wanted to leave, but it was late, too late to wake up Ariel and go out looking for a motel. And if we did that, it would hurt my father. I said, 'Honey, it's just for one night. Let's make the best of it, okay?'

"I woke up an hour or two later. I don't know how else to explain this. Maybe I was hallucinating. But Dolores, who's round, voluptuous, what Jewish people call *zaftig*, had grown. This very juicy, buxom blue-eyed blond was now ten, maybe twelve feet tall and growing bigger by the second. Her breasts and arms were gone. She had become a pythoness and she seemed to be shedding her skin, and I knew I was the skin she was shedding. She was gazing off into space. The Dolores I had known was gone. The creature beside me had no personality, no consciousness. Something possessed her, had taken her over. Whatever it was, I knew if that "thing" became aware I was watching, it would coil itself around me. Suffocate me.

"I pretended to be asleep. In fact, I forced myself to go back to sleep. I didn't want to see, I didn't want to know what Dolores or that thing that possessed her was doing. To this day I don't know if Dolores knew what was happening that night. I felt somehow weakened during that visit and that I had unknowingly introduced a pythonic being into my father's home. I remember thinking, Who in Skokie knows how to deal with such a python? Even afterwards, doctor, I was too scared to tell her I had had this hallucination. And I hope it was only an hallucination.

"Such a light woman she seemed. Before we married I raved about her to my friends. For me, in the beginning, Dolores Divine was golden, ample. Emotionally stable. Even her family name, *Norishen*, before her father changed it, meant 'to nourish, to keep alive.' In the 1940s, before she was born, her father changed *Norishen* to Divine. O Dolores, O Dolores Divine.

"In America, people say 'It takes one to know one.' Maybe there's a ten-foot python or cobra in me. Don't you teach that we all have untapped energy, a coiled serpent, at the base of our spines, a true goddess by our genitals, the unawakened *kundalini*? Could I have been witness to the awakening of Dolores' kundalini? Maybe I was blind, repressive, fearful and the child of middle-class Jews.

"Doctor, I'm more conventional than what your chalkboard might lead you to think. And after five marriages, I find each divorce hurts just as much, maybe more, than the one before."

THE AIM OF YOGA IS UNION WITH THE SELF. SEX IS NOT UNION.

"What about soulmates?" Noah asks.

SOULS DON'T MATE, writes the doctor.

13

Menage a Trois

"Well, how about a subscription to the *Saturday Evening Post* and a *menage a trois*?" said Dolores at dinner one evening during the reign of Richard Nixon.

His fork midway to his open mouth, Noah wondered what was coming next. To his amazement, the hairs in his nostrils had suddenly quivered and snapped to attention.

"Do you have someone in mind, Dee?" he asked, pouring more wine. A dreamy smile on his face, speaking softly so Dee could not hear, he addressed the troublemaking stirrings in his chest and groin, the death–defying cardio-vascular system somersaulting at the prospect of simultaneous contact with two women. "Whoa," he commanded, "Whoa."

Twirling her little finger in the goblet, raising it to her lips, Dolores sampled the Chardonnay.

"People say Vancouver is culturally oppressed, but I'm liking it more and more," she said. "The daffodils. The bakeries...It's feminine, a safe haven."

"It's a redneck city without a center, a city without bookstores."

"It's nice even if there are no bookstores. It's pretty," Dolores pouted. "Professor MacLashen says Vancouver is one of the West Coast's magnets."

"What does magnet mean? There are black holes in space that work like magnets. They suck things in and they disappear forever," he said.

"Vancouver is not a black hole." Dolores banged on the table.

"How do you know? And what do you mean *pretty?*"

"You know," she said. "Pretty park. Pretty harbor. Pretty West Georgia Street. Pretty whores. Pretty drunks. I like living in the West End. Look at that view: Stanley Park, the ferry boats. Isn't that romantic?"

Noah nodded.

"Actually, I was thinking of my Canadian friend, Louise," she purred, extending her tongue to her wine-wet finger. "Louise says two is company and three's a crowd, unless you're married. Then three is company and two's a crowd."

"So, in your friend's view, menage a trois is wholesome company," Noah teased. "I wonder, what does that say about us?"

"We're an old married twosome, a crowd."

"When did she say that?"

"At dinner last week, remember? Louise and Charles that English surfer. 'Sweet Louise,' you called her 'Sweet Louise.' Imagine that. Noah, you're blushing."

"She's an enchantress," Noah sighed. He'd played footsies with Louise, she of the jetty skin and mask-like smile, while Dolores and the Englishman argued the pros and cons of legalizing hemp.

"Yeah, umm, well, she's a knockout. I like all your friends, Dolores. How do you like the salad? More honey-cilantro dressing?"

"Oh, Noah, come off it! You were flirting with her."

"Okay, okay. I'm guilty. But really, we were just teasing one another, touching antennae. Getting it on with Louise is something else. More pasta? A little hollandaise for your salmon?"

"Just wine. You are interested, aren't you Noah? Well, I'll tell you something. Louise is attracted to you. And you're in luck."

"How do you figure?"

"She's my type too."

"Uh huh. In my limited experience..."

"Your limited experience? I know all about your limited experience. Noah, you'll like it with Louise. You'll like it. That is, if that old firehose of yours is up to it. Is that it? Is that what you're afraid of?"

"What is this, a test? Alright. Alright. But you want to know something? I care enough about you, Dolores, to be glad you're going to be there."

"That's sweet. Tell me more."

"I think a threesome that includes one's spouse is an improvement on sneaking off somewhere and then making up all sorts of stories."

"Noah, I can see your tongue hanging out."

"Let me finish. Seriously, if I happen to step out on someone, the guilt factor, having to lie and cheat, poisons the relationship. Lying and cheating are a pain in the ass."

"That never stopped you in the past."

"Maybe not, but I still felt guilty. I'm not one of those people who gets turned on by intrigue. Anyway, I want our marriage to work."

"So do I. What do you think about that? And an open marriage is an honest marriage," she said. "Sex without guilt. Think about it. You get your desserts and you get to eat them at home too. Are you ready for coffee?"

Pouring, Dolores sang off key, "*That was a very good year...* Noah, baby, do you know that Frank Sinatra song?"

"*That was a very good year...* Sounds to me like a wine commercial, but it must have to do with romance."

"That's right," Dolores said, unbuttoning his shirt.

"All right, Dee. Say we include Louise. Who do we include next time? I'm not sharing you with another man. Chalk it up to age, but I've come to think screwing around is for screwballs."

"Noah, did it ever occur to you that you might unconsciously be making me set up this threesome? Think of it, your wife and her best friend in the same bed: Louise on your left, me on your right. I know you've thought of it, Noah. It's every man's fantasy. You're the one who really wants it, not me."

"Good try, Dee, but I don't think so."

"Men are such hypocrites! When we first met you described yourself as 'an adventurous, self-involved seeker with a streak of the screwball.'"

"That's true, Dee, but you're leaving something out. I also said I was in the process of shedding my screwed-up-ness."

"Noah, baby, we're two of a kind. Look," she said, touching his knee, "we've been together about four years, right? It's time to loosen up. You know what your problem is? You take marriage too seriously. Really, you're too much into marriage."

"And you see an orgy as the solution to my being too much into marriage?"

"Just think of our threesome, our sharing Louise, as an experiment."

"Sharing your Canadian friend. God, it sounds as if we're talking about joint ownership of a sailboat or two lions feasting on an antelope. Mmm, say I agreed..."

"Say you agreed? You've already agreed."

"That's wishful thinking. I haven't agreed to anything."

"That's what you say," she answered.

"Dee, if it takes two to tango, what do you call a threesome?" he asked, lighting a joint.

"A conundrum? A triangle? I don't know, Mr. Smart Guy, what would you call it?"

"A puzzlement. Anyway, this time the guilt factor is not going to be a problem. Right, Dolores? We're not going to have to hide anything. And if we split, it's not going to be because I did something behind your back."

"Well, you do know there are people who have sex outside the menage a trois. Even that's not enough for them."

"There are springboards into marriage and there are springboards out of marriage. Anyway Dee, you have my word. Do I have yours?"

"We'll see," she said, reaching for the joint.

Satisfied she had him hooked, Dolores upped the ante.

"Later, if it turns out you want more than two sweethearts at a time, let me know. But in fairness, I think we should include one or two men, too."

"Is that what this is all about?" Noah pushed away his plate.

"Calm yourself, honey. Can't you see I'm joking? Anyway, we need to think. A threesome takes planning. And at least one of us has to know something about choreography and set design." Standing, Dolores did a little cha-cha.

"And etiquette. I'll write a letter to Miss Manners," Noah said.

"That's right. Ask about how to host an orgy—trains and daisy chains. I know what Miss Manners will tell you: 'Dear Daisy Chain, No hidden cameras, no one-way mirrors, no tape recorders.'"

"Did you think I was planning on selling tickets?"

14

Worn Out Poppa Blues

Vancouver, British Columbia

5:00 P.M. — THE SHOWER

Reaching down to soap his manager, Noah considered disappearing, going AWOL for the evening—catching a ballgame, watching a movie. Instead he listened as his adviser, Homerun Harold, purple of face, veiny of neck, reviewed the nature of the evening's affair.

"You have no choice," said Harold. If you don't agree, your wife is going to step out on you. You know that. She'll touch base with every player on the West Coast. I've done all I can for you, Newmark. Two, three times a day sometimes, drunk or sober, but she's restless. It's ironic, isn't it?"

"What do you mean *ironic?* "Noah asked.

"You doing a threesome and all in order to stay with her. Well, Dolores wants a little excitement, but who doesn't? You have to hand it to her. In one respect at least it's a good thing, promising," said the one-eyed manager.

"What do you see as promising?" Noah asked, massaging conditioner into his hair.

"I mean Dolores is inviting you to join her in an affair. She's hoping to play around as much as she can and, at the same time, keep you happy and available. You want the marriage to work and I guess she does too. Isn't that promising?"

"Marriage? You call this a marriage? This is a farce. We've been through this before, Harold. This marriage is in deep shit."

"What can I say? Hang in there. Try it for a while. See if you can keep up with her. What was it your father used to say: 'Everytime you're with a woman, send her someplace she's never been before.' She wants something new, give her something new. Play along. Who knows, maybe this time she's going to send us someplace we've never been before. What a kick, eh?"

"Yeah, that's what I'm afraid of," Noah said.

"Score one for the Borscht Belt. But really, you can count on me. One woman, two women, no problem. I'm not some clever comic, but if I'm up to bat and have a woman on base, I'm gonna bring her and her friends on home and I'm gonna do it the way they like best," said his dick.

"Oh, shut up. Save it for the reporters. Can't you let go of your need to impress people?"

Chastened, Harold nodded and turned away.

"Okay, Noah said, "suppose, just suppose it plays out the way we want it to. Dee and I still have to do something to pull the marriage together. Either we re-connect or the marriage dissolves.

"...Louise has to have an agenda of her own," Noah said, rinsing himself. "Did you ever think of that? Scattershot, shooting without aiming, isn't going to work this time. And you, when was the last time you even had an agenda? 'Send it into deep center field, score now to left field, come on, bring it on home,' that's all you think."

"And look at you, Newmark, with all your smarts, you're still talking to your pecker. Do you know what that makes you? You're one of those guys who thinks with his schmuck and fucks with his mind. Yeah, it's true, isn't it? You're the prick, not me."

"Is someone in there with you, Noah? Who are you talking to?"

"Dee, where'd you come from? And you're smoking again, aren't you? Damn, I've got soap in my eyes," Noah said, pulling open the shower curtain. "C'mon, honey take your robe off and get in here!"

"It's so steamy I can't even see," she wailed, feeling with her foot, stepping inside with him. "Noah, dear, would you soap my back? Oh, rub me now with the washcloth. Use the loofa. Harder. Hmm. What's that?" she said, feeling something poke at her back.

"You know what that is."

"Oh, I see. How are tricks, Harold? What are you up to lately?" she said, kneeling as if to pet an animal. "Down, boy. Stop that! C'mon, Noah, save it for later."

"He just wants to play, Dee."

"Get serious. I need to ask you something," she said, throwing the marijuana joint into the sink. "What if Louise wants to stay a second night, or longer? We may never get rid of her. What then? You do understand, don't you, you're going to have to share your bathroom with Louise?"

"My bathroom? Why?" Noah asked, turning to give her the full spray.

"You know me," Dee said, "my bathroom's my sanctuary."

"You are a little strange, Dolores. I mean, I'm insulted. You're willing to share me with Louise, but not your bathroom."

"Share a bathroom with your lover and it takes away the mystery. That bathroom is my chapel, my temple of beauty. That's why we have two bathrooms.

"Besides, Noah, men are messy. They don't clean up after themselves. They leave the toilet seat up. They don't hang up the towels right."

"But Louise isn't like that," Noah said. "She's a woman."

"Some women are obsessive about cooking and won't allow anyone else into their kitchen. Well, I'm like that about my bathroom. I won't share it with anyone."

"I don't get it. If we're going to sleep together in one bed, why can't we shower together in one shower? Louise is trim, boyish even, with little boobies. She'd fit in here just fine. I've never showered with two women," Noah said.

"Anyway, why don't you and Louise go rent a motel room? You don't need me," Dee said, punching him in the chest. "She's exotic and thin. Isn't that what you like?"

"Whaat? Dolores, you're crazy," Noah laughed, grabbing her wrist before she could punch him again. "Tonight's little party was your idea. Look, it's okay. If you're having second thoughts I'll call her up and cancel." Noah stepped out of the shower and reached for his towel.

"No, it's too late. Louise will be here any minute. Oh, God, I don't know why I agreed to this. Hug me, hug me," she said turning off the shower.

Lips in her hair, his eyes burning, Noah embraced her.

"You're the one who set this up, weren't you, Noah?" she said as he trimmed his beard. "You're the one who wanted it." Dee let fly with another punch. "I care for you, Noah. Remember that. I care for you. I just want to let loose with other people now and then."

"I don't want to lose you," he whispered.

"I don't want to lose you either. But look, I'm gaining weight. See...Oh, God, what am I going to wear?" Dee cried, heading for her closet.

6:00 P.M. — THE PARTY

"That's the doorbell," Dee said, as Noah pulled on a pair of Levis. "Noah, you let her in. No, I'll go.

"...Oh, Louise, Louise, how thoughtful! What beautiful

flowers. And I like you with your hair like that, down over your shoulders..." The two women embraced.

Feeling an intruder, Noah held back.

"Noah," his wife called, "Look who's here, honey."

"Surprise, surprise," said Noah under his breath.

"Hi, Louise." Pacing himself, anxious not to appear over-eager, Noah hugged Louise. About to withdraw, he stood transfixed as she stepped back, raised her skirt and offered him a glimpse of forbidden treasure, a shock of poussay topped by a fluorescent pink, heart-shaped beaver.

"Yes, yes, Louise. I'll be right back."

Suppressing an urge to pop in one of his audiotapes and record the proceedings, Noah went to the fridge to retrieve the Chardonnay he'd bought for the occasion. He gathered up the goblets, poured for the women and, like an anxious stage director, checked the bedroom to make sure the massage oil and flower-scented candles were in place.

Would he be up to satisfying Louise—and Dolores? It wouldn't be easy, but he knew he had to try to be more of a team player, one who sacrificed his needs to advance the needs of others, one who found satisfaction in doing all he could to make his teammates shine, who found pleasure in their pleasure, delight in their delight, success in their success.

He'd get his kicks after they got theirs. He'd spend the evening building up steam, then clear the bases with one or the other in the early hours of the morning. A recovery period would follow and, God willing, he'd clear the bases again. But what if, for some reason, he lost control? Or popped out the first time he came up to bat?

For all his boasting, there were times when Harold was lucky to make it to first base. And of course there was a danger in overcompensating, in relying too much on technique. The women Noah had known tended to protest when they sensed he was relying more on nimble-fingered craft than heart. "Who taught you to touch a woman like that? Did you read about it somewhere?" they asked suspiciously.

Planning to control himself in one respect, Noah was unable to control himself in another. Realized fantasy or not, he stopped at his desk and scribbled

> Hosting a threesome, a critique of triangles:
>
> 1) A man loses interest in his lover and she introduces a second woman into the relationship in order to make him happy. Sorry, wrong scenario.
>
> 2) Seeing her husband is on the verge of getting together with her best friend, the wife preempts the affair by offering him simultaneous sex with the other woman and herself. By taking the initiative in this way, she manages to control the action.
>
> 3) Two passionate women, attracted to one another, but not wanting to think of themselves as gay, decide to include a man. Perhaps.
>
> 4) As an opening wedge, a friend insinuates herself into a couple's bed and steals whichever one of the two she most desires: a) the man, b) the woman. Maybe she wants c) both the man and the woman.
>
> 5) Three voyeurs agree to have a threesome in order to get their kicks (as spectators). Among other things, threesome sex is an experiment in voyeurism. One gets to be a voyeur of the other two, but also of oneself.

6) BEST is when no one is a voyeur. BEST is when all three are actively participating.

"Honey, would you bring out the rest of the hors d'oeuvres?"

"Oh, and more wine too," Louise called from the bedroom. "Where's that Chardonnay from?"

"Do you like it? It's from California—Sonoma County," Noah called back, grabbing the cork screw.

Rejoining the women, refilling their glasses, Noah turned to the tape deck. He put on Bessie Smith's *Any Woman's Blues* with Bessie singing *I'm Wild About That Thing*; *My Love Comes Down*; and *Worn Out Poppa Blues*.

"Hey, Noah, c'mon," Louise said after *Worn Out Poppa*, "let's hear some rock and roll. Enough of the heavy stuff."

"I've got just the man for you," he said putting on Elvis Presley's *Love Me Tender*.

Next, Noah turned his attention to the bedroom fireplace. Threw on more dry cedar chips and logs. As the fire blazed, he helped Louise remove her quilted leather jacket. Catching Noah's eye, she unzipped and kicked off her highheeled boots. Noah then, watchful, calmed himself by sipping wine and massaging Dolores' instep and ankles.

"Louise, I got some really good hash from my hairdresser," said Dee. "Would you like to try some?"

"Sure, why not?" she said, removing her glasses. "It's gonna be a long night. Oh, what a beautiful pipe!"

"It's new," Noah said. "Smoking's healthier this way. You can smoke more without messing up your throat. Bongs remove the toxins and the water cools the smoke...I did an article on bongs. They're also called *hubble-bubbles*."

"Oh, there he goes again, Mr. Encyclopedia," Dee said.

Louise and Noah watched as Dee added water and ice to the glass chamber.

"Glass gives you the cleanest hit," Noah said.

Inserting aluminum foil in the seat of the bowl, Dolores poked at it a few times with a sewing needle so the pipe would draw. Next, crumbling a chunk of brownie-black hash with her thumb and middle finger, she deposited the resin on the foil. Handing the pipe to Louise, she watched as her friend brought the mouthpiece to her lips.

"Ready?"

Holding the pipe, leaning forward for the match, she nodded.

"Whew, that smells like camel shit," she giggled, passing the pipe back to Dee. Then, as Dee held the pipe, Louise put a second and a third match to the resin.

"What's better, one water chamber or two?" Lou asked, her dark eyes shining.

"A single chamber, like this," said Noah. "It's easier to clean."

"Noah's into 'bong hygiene,'" Dee snickered.

"Is a bigger bong better?" Lou asked, letting out her breath.

"It's a matter of personal preference," Noah laughed. "What do you think, Dee?"

Leaning forward, Dee kissed Louise flush on the lips.

"All I know is with a good water pipe, there's no waste," Dee said, toasting Noah and Lou.

Noah's turn. Two or three puffs and he saw his father in 3-D: "So, Sonny, you got yourself invited to a picnic. May you enjoy in good health. Of course, a man's shortcomings he can hide from one woman, but two? Excuse me for laughing, but these friends of yours are in a league of their own."

"Louise, I have a question for you," Noah said, reaching for the Brie spreading dreamily across the cheeseboard.

"I'll give you the answer first."

"What's your answer?" Noah asked.

"No," laughed Louise.

"Actually, it's a question about three-sies. I don't want you or Dee to be hurt in this," Noah said.

"Right."

"Louise, threesomes are unstable, aren't they? I can't help thinking: When two kids are friends and a third kid comes along, sometimes all three play together. But eventually two gang up on one and that one is left out. One of us could end up feeling hurt."

"We haven't even started, Newmark, and you're telling me one of us is going to be sent home early?" Louise frowned and held out her wine goblet for a refill.

"Noah's one of those sensitive, considerate men who like to control everything. Honey, please, just for tonight, forget you're a teacher," Dee said, touching his lips. Louise and I know you don't want anyone to be hurt. But you're the man, you're in charge. Things can go any way you want them to."

"Am I really in charge, Dee? You and Divine Mother Kali—and me? I don't think so."

"He has a point. We do out-number him," Louise chuckled.

"You're the center of attention, Noah," Dee said, snuggling with Louise. "See?" she said as the two women looked him over. "We're just checking you out, and you pass. C'mon, honey, lighten up."

"Yeah," said Louise, taking another toke of hash, "and even if one of us is odd man out that person still gets to watch what the other two are doing, okay? We don't send anyone home early— no matter what. In my opinion, voyeurism is a lost art."

Noah and Dolores turned their attention to Louise.

"Are you warm enough, Lou? Here, let me help you off

with your top," Dolores offered. Now you can join the party. Here, take my seat," she said, surrendering her place on the bed. "Let me paint your toenails and Noah—he studied massage, you know—can do your neck and shoulders."

"Oh, God, I love it. Mmm, that's great."

"Hey, you guys," said their guest, tongue moistening her lips, "what's up with you two?"

"Louise, really, we're getting along fine. Noah here is just gonna loosen up a little, aren't you honey? You know, we've been married for four years. There's a lot out there we wanna try," said Dolores.

"You want to add a little spice to your relationship, is that it?" said Louise. "Someone to stir the pot? Hmm. Tell me, Noah, how do you feel about that?"

Noah grimaced. "How do I feel about that? How do I feel about that? I'm here, aren't I? You sound like some kind of shrink. But yeah, we belong together, Louise. I love my wife."

"Love is for sissies." Louise laughed. "By the way, once you've done a menage a trois, there's no going back," she said, running her hands through her hair. "The marriage changes. It's one of those things."

"We want to enlarge our circle of friends, become more intimate with one or two special people," Dee added.

"Noah, are you prepared to compromise?" Louise asked, slipping easily into the role of marriage counselor. An expression of honest concern on her face, at once fatalistic and lustful, accepting and lascivious, she provided Noah and Dolores one last opportunity to withdraw.

It was a classy maneuver, one that increased Noah's respect for his wife's friend.

"Noah, I understand you support threesomes, but you're not so sure about open marriage," she went on.

"I am sure about it. I'm against open marriage," said Noah.

"Oh, I see. You don't think a threesome is open marriage?" Louise said.

"Noah doesn't think a threesome with you is the same as open marriage." Dolores reached for Louise's hand. "Did you know Noah has the hots for you? Really, Lou, whatever happens is our problem. We won't think about that now, okay?

"Noah, darling, we're yours. What's your pleasure...?" Dee asked.

His head spinning, unable to make sense of what Dee was doing with her mouth, Noah kissed the back of Louise's neck. To his surprise, the palm of his hand rested lightly on his wife's breast. Dee, meanwhile, nibbled and bit Louise's neck and ears.

Sitting up, his mouth open, Noah listened as the women kissed.

"You're beautiful, both of you. I don't know why you want to bother making love to a man," Noah said. "I mean, women are so much better at it. At least I think I'm learning something."

"Learning what?" Louise snorted.

"Before you go any further with that thing," Lou said as he approached, "before you touch me or your wife, I want you to repeat after me, 'Poussy makes the world go round.'"

"Why?" Noah asked.

"Because it isn't often women get to hear men speak the truth."

Sniffing her perfume, Irish heather, Irish moss, Noah felt a circuit close down in his brain.

Noah hesitated as she kneeled before him.

"You'll have to speak up!"

"Poussy makes the world go round," Noah said.

"I accept you as my student," she said, leaning forward to receive him.

"Lou, you're outrageous," Dee said, undoing her bra as she advanced. "Who would have thought? In that gallery of yours, with your glasses and your hair pulled back, you're pure business...I mean..."

"Now, how would you like to demonstrate your fondness for Irish heather? Think, Noah," said Louise.

Headlights. Voices. Car doors opening and closing. *KNOCK, KNOCK.*

"Who's there?" said Noah.

'God, that hashish has really gotten to me. What if this were all about to be recorded?'

"Mr. Newmark, I'm Mike Wright of 39 Minutes. Can I ask you a few questions?" said the newsman, pushing his way into the room.

"Questions? What questions?" Noah asked.

"Your friend Louise Pettigrew informed us...She invited..."

The crew from *39 Minutes* rushed past Noah with lights and camera equipment.

"Ladies and gentlemen," said Mike Wright, *"we're in Vancouver, Canada, with an expatriate journalist; Dolores, his spirited wife; and their friend, Louise Pettigrew, the owner of Pettigrew Contemporary Art."*

"Tell us, Noah, what does this twisted behavior make you feel like?" asked 39 Minutes.

"What ...feels like? Feels great, Mike. Once you got into it, it's the most...natural thing in the world," he said, turning back to Dee.

"Yeah, Mike...you don't know...what...you're missing," Dolores added, burrowing under the sheet.

"For those of you who may have tuned in late, this is Mike Wright reporting live from the bedside...of Mr. and Mrs. Newmark..."

"Mrs. Newmark? What an assumption," said Dee. "Dolores. Dolores Divine's the name."

"There he is now on his knees...Noah's like a caboose...the trainman's car...in this affair.

"Lovemaking can be as mysterious and dangerous as..."

"Actually, Mike...it's a mingling of intimate knowledge and surprise," offered Louise.

Firelight, candlelight, light show, daisy chain. Nibble ...lick...bite...squeeze...pant...suck...moan...

One, two, three. A, B, C.
Do it to her, do it to me.
Ease back slowly now.
Ah, bravissimo! Magnifico!

"Noah, how would you justify this kind of behavior?" Mike Wright broke in. *"And...isn't that...a hash pipe I see over there?"*

"Well, um...it's like...like a wedding night...with two brides," Noah answered, Dee's teddy bears—all five of his wives collected teddy bears—bouncing up and down on the creaky bed, sweat running into his eyes, the teddy bears blurring... "It's the scent of sandalwood and honeyed cinnamon...two mouths, three mouths, one mouth...Uh, uh, O Louise, mmm, mmm." Noah writhed between them. "That's it Dee, yess, yess..." he cried, falling out of bed with the women.

"How do you handle boundary negotiations?" Mike Wright came in close with his microphone.

"See Noah, wasn't I right?" said Dee.

"I've never been so busy in my life," Noah answered.

"Boundary negotiations? Hmm. I don't know, Mike," Noah whispered. "It's complicated...sometimes...it can be a little lonely...okay, Louise, just...just a minute...No, no thanks, Dolores, that's okay...It's hard to be there 100% for one woman, or she for you...it's even harder..."

"Could you tell us...briefly...Dolores...what's it like for you?" said Wright.

"Uh, uh...it's like a trio of billiard balls clicking—each setting off the other," Dolores said.

"Do you agree or disagree with that description, Noah?" said Mike Wright.

"Well, the women...uh, uh, are doubled...in a sense, uh, uh, and the man is...uh, doubled too, or at least...O, God, honey, don't move!...he feels doubled, too. I feel...I could...make love...to one...hundred women...at..."

"You feel invincible?"

"Hey, we're just...having...fun..."

❖❖❖

3:30 A.M. — WINDING DOWN

"Well, Noah, are you pleased with yourself?" said Dee.

"Whew," said Noah, head back, legs rubbery, gasping for breath.

"There, there, you'll be okay," Dee teased. "But tell me something. Honestly. Were you really there or were you writing a scenario? Men fantasize...so do women...And you've said the ultimate fantasy for men, some men, is to have sex with two women, simultaneously. Okay, here you are in bed with two beautiful women. What did you fantasize this time? Did you think of other...partners...did it add to the excitement? The truth, Noah!"

"Uh, uh...I fantasized...doing...what we did...but doing it...on national television. In Canada. And the U.S.," Noah confessed.

"Noah is perverse," said Dee, turning to Louise. "If this man were being interviewed on television, he'd answer the questions, but at the same time he'd fantasize about threesomes."

"All that's wrong with Noah is an overactive imagination," said Louise, coming to his defense.

15

Menage a Trois
Day 4

6:00 A.M.

Head aching, Noah woke to find the spousal bed filled to capacity. Slipping away from the sleeping women, bleary-eyed, he tiptoed to the kitchen where he put on a pot of coffee. At noon he'd have to lecture to that Introduction to Journalism class. Yawning, stretching, he threw back a vitamin capsule, and glared at a pile of fifty unmarked papers. Peeling an apple, reading the first, he scrawled "Too much of a good thing. Crowded with ideas."

"Claustrophobic situation. Open it up more," he wrote on another, the scent of sweet musk and salmon on his bathrobe.

"Have you thought this out completely? Your essay pivots on a slippery premise. Where are you really going with this?" he wrote on a third.

For four hours he went through the set of essays. "The situation you describe is unstable." "Something's wrong here." "Something's got to give."

At 10 A.M., all the papers graded, he opened the fridge and began to prepare breakfast. Thirty minutes later he entered the bedroom with a tray of fresh-squeezed orange juice, hot buttered croissants, strawberry jam and coffee.

"What men don't know...Oh, hi, Noah...breakfast in bed,

how sweet," said Louise. "You're making a tradition of it, you know. You sure you don't mind?"

"I need time alone in the morning, Lou...now more than ever," he added under his breath. "Heating up some croissants is a small price to pay. Really, mornings are my thinking time."

"Maybe you need a little breather, Noah." Dee smiled.

"What men don't know," said Lou, turning back to Dolores, "is that women who scarcely know one another...who've just met...will agree on one thing for starters...and that's that men are not to be trusted, that they're unreliable."

"Here you have one adoring man bringing you breakfast in bed...and for some reason you're trashing him. I must have missed something," Noah protested.

"Okay, okay, you're right. Present company excepted," Lou assured him.

"Hmm. You know, Lou, you're right," Dee said, reaching for a croissant. "I mean the deck...is stacked against us...only exceptional women...can put the system to their advantage," she continued, croissant in one hand, coffee in the other."

"It all comes down to sex," Lou said. "Women are more naturally promiscuous than men. And that is why men do all they can to control women, why they make laws and things, to rein them in, turn them into property."

"What men don't know is that women do their emotional work for them," said Dee, as Noah reached to put his hand over her mouth. "Am I right? Most men don't feel. Noah's an exception. It's women who interact in the world for them."

Sitting on the side of the bed, crumpling the newspaper, Noah turned to the women. "I feel like the lone male at a pajama party."

Seeing what she took to be a smile, Dee upbraided her mate.

"Ah, the doubly privileged male," she said, dropping buttery flakes on the bed sheet.

"Yeah, Noah, how come you never shop or clean up after yourself? I'm not sure I like what I've been hearing," said Louise.

"Look, Lou, if Dee has something to say about my domestic habits, she can say it for herself."

"Well, I'll say it then, Noah. You don't do your share," said Dolores.

"Maybe you guys should re-negotiate your expectations of each other," Lou suggested.

"You know, Lou, you sound more and more like Dee's mother."

"What do you mean my mother?" Dee asked.

"It was fun with just you and Louise. Now it's my wife and mother-in-law in the same bed."

"Double the pleasure, double the fun," said Louise.

"Double the pain, double the grief," Noah grumbled.

"Look, I don't like what I'm hearing," said Louise, running naked into the bathroom to shower.

"What is it with you, Noah?" Dee asked. "Oh, don't give me that helpless 'woe-is-me' look," she said, as Noah prepared to leave. "See, Lou, what did I tell you? Is this a moody chauvinist, or not? Look at him, he's thinking, 'What did I do now?'" Dee said.

"Well, at least he prepared breakfast, which is more than most men do," Louise said, brushing her hair.

Menage a Trois — Day 6

7:00 A.M.

> "Sonofabitch. Living with two women under one roof is more demanding than having one in one place and one in another," Noah scribbled in his notebook. "It's a relief to get away from them...to be on my own for an hour..."

I once thought of a threesome as energy-efficient: a form of car-pooling.

Thoreau says, 'It takes two to speak the truth—one to speak, and another to hear.' When I hold Dee in my arms and tell her exactly what I'm thinking— and hear her do the same—I get turned on.

But there's a risk. The risk is getting thrown out of bed or kicked in the head. Booted from the pleasure garden for owning up to ...for simply saying what you're feeling.

Menage a Trois – Day 9

Up at dawn, slipping into the kitchen, Noah dialed his first wife, Shelley, in Chicago.

"Hello, Shelley? Are you busy?"

"Oh, Noah...I can tell from your voice...What's wrong? No, let me guess. You and Dolores..."

"How did you...? Yes, Dolores. And Louise. Louise Pettigrew." Noah told her about the menage a trois.

"I come home from a hard day of teaching and instead of being fussed over...the women gang up on me."

"You went for high stakes...marrying a *Kama Sutra* centerfold with brains..."

"Sometimes I wish Dee and Louise would go off on their own and...leave me out of it."

"Well, what were you expecting? Noah and his lady loves."

"Expecting...? I thought having everything in the open

would make it okay. Remember that scene in Fellini's *8½* where Mastroianni sees his wife and mistress walking together arm-in-arm?"

"Part of your problem, Noah, is that you connect sex with marriage. You're naive. There aren't many men who sleep with a woman and then think they have to marry her. Have you ever had sex with someone you didn't consider marrying?"

"A couple times, maybe."

"Oh, great! And I was dumb enough to marry you," Shelley cried.

"Noah, I wanted to tell you...on television...There was this woman who had been married eleven times. She's like you. She just believes in marriage. On average her marriages last about one year. One guy she was married to lasted three hours. I don't know how she does it," Shelley said. "I can't think of eleven men I've ever wanted to be with."

"Do you remember her name? I'd like to interview her, do a story."

"Ask her out? Seriously, Noah, why not do a feature on hit-and-run marriages?"

"Hit-and-run marriages?"

"Hit-and-run brides, hit-and-run couples. Michelle Phillips and Dennis Hopper stayed married for about eight days. Ethel Merman and Ernest Borgnine...twenty-one days. Gloria Swanson and Wallace Beery...less than a month."

"You remind me of myself with your memory for trivia," Noah laughed.

"Let's get back to your menage a trois, Noah. That's why you called, isn't it?"

"Yeah."

"What do you think Louise wants, Noah?"

"I think if it were possible, Louise would like us to adopt her.

Last night Dee and I went to bed early. We thought we were being quiet. Lou has a room of her own. Anyway, that's where Lou was when she began crying, in the guest room. Really, why can't she let Dolores and me alone sometimes? This isn't what I expected. I thought she was a strong, independent woman. Where did this needy child come from?"

"She's settled in and won't let you two be alone? Mmm. It sounds to me like she's up to no good," said Shelley.

"And what do you think Dolores wants?" Shelley asked.

"Dolores sees herself as a superstar in a movie with a cast of thousands. Honestly, Shelley, I don't think she's written in a starring role for me."

"There's a word for people like Louise."

"What's that?" Noah asked.

"Triangulator, a person who gets off on the heat of triangles. One-on-one sex may not turn her on," said Shelley. "The excitement of a threesome, a crowd, that's what gets a triangulator going.

"Maybe you're just having trouble keeping up with the women in your life."

"What do you mean?"

"You know that Mort Sahl joke: in the fifties you had to be a Jew to get a girl. In the sixties you had to be black to get a girl. Now you have to be a girl to get a girl."

"You're joking, aren't you, Shelley? Dee's..."

"Look, I don't think Dolores is going to let up on her open marriage *shtick*. They say the cuckolded husband is the last to find out. I don't think so. The cuckold is the first to know. It's just that to protect himself from the pain of knowing, he pretends for as long as he can. That's what I've done. And that's why Dolores was so anxious for me to get together with Louise. It takes the pressure off."

"Goodbye marriage number three," Shelley said gently.

"Shelley, honey, did you ever get that questionnaire I sent? You know, the one that asks what was it like for you when we were married?"

"Of course. The much-marrying man's Gallup poll—surveying his ex-spouses to see how he tests out. Checking out how his former wives feel about moral and social issues of the day. I'm happy to be your confidante, but I'm not going to answer those fucking questions."

Noah's Questionnaire:

Dear Shelley/Anna:

Please reply to any or all of the following. Add anything else you care to.

1. What attracted you, what made you agree to get married in the first place?
2. What were your ideals about marriage before we married? After? What now?
3. One telling anecdote that summarizes our marriage?
4. What was the best of it?
5. What was the worst?
6. Funniest moment?
7. Moment when you knew it was over? Is there such a thing as an 'irrevocable' act which, having occurred, represents the turning point or end of a relationship?
8. When you talk about our marriage—assuming you do—what do you find yourself saying first? ('Yeah, I was married to a newspaperman...' etc.)
9. If a friend asked you for advice before marrying a writer, what would you say?

10. In your mind, what are the great moral and social issues of the day?

May I quote you if needed?

All my best,

Noah Newmark

"Noah, you sure have your nerve."

"Shelley, you used to say much-married people eventually get around to re-marrying one of their ex-spouses. I'm glad for you. I mean, that you've gotten your life together. I really am.

"But honey...I'm serious...if you were...available, I'd make a play for you. You're honest, you're straight and you know me really well. We wouldn't have to play any games."

"Noah, dear, you can't stand being without a woman, can you? Well, I'm flattered and I do still care for you. In fact, I care for you a lot, a lot more than when I was married to you. But once was enough, don't you think?"

"No, that's what I'm saying, Shelley. Once wasn't enough."

16

Marriage #4
Women, Children, Physicians & Kings

Mt. Chakra, The Santa Cruz Mountains,

1:00 P.M.

Under a tarpaulin outside the doctor's cabin, a half dozen singers and musicians playing tambura, sitar and harmonium chant hymns to the Goddess mother. *Jai Durga Lakshmi. Bhaja Ma Ma Ma Ma...*

"Why the hell don't they sing hymns to Apollo or Aphrodite?" Noah wants to know. "What's so special about Durga and Lakshmi? How do we know there isn't a Hellenic temple somewhere where devotees play the lyre and lute, or whatever the Greeks and Romans used to make music, and sing their hearts out to those gods?

Hail Apollo,
God of Light and Wisdom...

At that moment someone rings the commune's lunch bell. Rama, relaxed as when the session began, seems not to hear. Noah, glancing across at the doctor, refills the man's teacup.

The fragrance of incense mingles with that of ground ginger, cardamom, nutmeg and cloves.

"I won't have to go through this again sometime, will I?" Noah says, pouring himself a fresh cup of the sweet, milky tea.

Rama, expressionless, merely raises his eyebrows.

"You know, account for all my marriages. This is a once-and-for-all event, right?"

A look of amusement plays across Rama's face.

"Look, I know I've overdone it..." Noah says.

CONTINUE, the doctor writes, leaning back, his legs crossed.

"Okay then," Noah says, "on to number four."

YOU HAD ONE CHILD WITH DOLORES, Rama writes on his chalkboard.

Reminding himself to repeat aloud everything the doctor writes so he'll have it on tape, Noah speaks into the microphone at the same time he copies Rama's words into his notebook.

"Yes, my daughter Ariel." Checking the recorder, Noah pops out one cassette tape, labels it *Dr. R., side B* and inserts a new one.

Rama wipes the chalkboard with a white woolen thumb-sized eraser. Noah blinks and looks again.

Someone has shaped the eraser to resemble the teacher himself. How come he uses a little dummy of himself to do the clean-up?

Noah rubs his eyes.

"What's the story behind that finger puppet?" he asks.

Rama acknowledges the question with a smile.

The two men sit side by side on the sofa, the doctor with his wispy white beard and mustache and Noah with his own long red whiskers. Each watches the other.

"How could I have missed...that thing does look like you. It's a sort of homunculus, isn't it?"

ERASES KARMA, Rama writes, holding up the mannequin for inspection.

Wiping the board, the doctor turns again to Noah. Preoccupied, his eyes filling, Newmark speaks as much to himself as to Rama.

"Before we divorced, Dee had said, 'You'll be a better father to Ariel than I can be a mother...' and offered me custody.

I hesitated because Ariel was so young, but we were already very close.

"Then I remember Dee saying, 'Don't say I never gave you anything.' The next morning, while I was teaching, she and her boyfriend came with a moving van—took all the dishes, the tables and chairs...everything except the books."

The doctor removes his glasses.

YOU RAISED ARIEL? he writes.

"Yes. I liked being father and mother...Natural childbirth, being there when Ariel was born, helped me connect with her in a way I wish I'd done with all my children...

"For a year I hardly dated. If I could, I'd have waited longer, but Ariel needed a real mother, and not just the people I hired to help out, but someone who might love her as I did. And I was lonely and had come to see...I was guilty, Rama, guilty for the hell I'd put my kids through."

Noah blinks.

The doctor's image fades and is replaced by that of a weaver seated at her loom. In Noah's eyes the loom resembles a musical instrument, a cello—'In weaving, you create your surface from scratch and build layers on top. Weaving is unforgiving. You can't subtract if you make a mistake,' Natasha explains, her hands spinning patterns in the air. Her words are threads which she has to pull and adjust...to the accompaniment of treadle and beater. Barefoot, a rosy-cheeked blonde, the weaver is wearing a gray tee-shirt and a pair of jeans. Pausing at the loom, her eyes closed, she sings,

Somewhere the moon is bright,
the night air warm,
the sea holds across the horizon
like a soft full sheet,
and it's time...

'Do you know Pushkin's poems?' she asks.

"O Natasha, honey, you're back," he says.

NATASHA, WIFE NUMBER FOUR... Rama writes.

"Huh? Yeah, right. Natasha Kaminsky. Sorry. I lost it there for a minute.

"Her mom was gone and Ariel would wake up at night screaming. I'd hold her and want to scream too. Eventually Ariel would fall back asleep with her eyes open and then she'd wake up and cry some more and say, 'Daddy, daddy, why do you say you have to work all the time?'

"When I got an assignment to cover the Montreal Film Festival, I didn't want to go. I felt guilty and didn't want to leave Ariel. But Dee agreed to look after her for that week and Ariel seemed to intuit...before I left she said, 'Daddy, promise you'll bring me back a present...No, no,' she said, 'someone to play with.'

"Jay Novak, an old writing buddy, invited me...'With this film festival happening, you're not going to be able to find a room. I've got a friend, Natasha,' he said. 'She's going to be away and says you can stay in her studio.'

"The studio was one of those loft spaces—big and airy with a skylight. I remember there was a samovar and the place smelled of cinnamon and wet yarn. It was filled with tapestries, rugs, and pillows she'd sewn with Russian peasant faces...and a loom made of walnut.

"During the day I watched movies, twenty in one week, and interviewed the filmmakers. Evenings I partied with Jay and the other writers.

"Then I'd go back to her room. It was otherworldly at night, like a deserted bazaar.

"By the fifth day I couldn't stop thinking about her or the whimsical, Old World women's faces she made. 'Novak,' I said,

'I want to know more about Natasha. Is she—with someone? I...I want to meet her.'

"He laughed. 'I see, you're ready to step back into the ring. Well, don't say I didn't warn you. Natasha's beautiful. You'll see for yourself, Newmark. Beautiful, in her mid-30's, and she works at being plain. She thinks people won't take her seriously unless she wears glasses and keeps her hair pulled back. At the same time she enjoys playing the innocent greenhorn...the big round-faced Russian doll.

"'Dee was glamorous, shapely, but Natasha's the mad artist and substantial, like one of Bruegel's peasants.

"One day you'll learn, Newmark. Yeah,' he said, 'I'll introduce you.'

"Natasha returned and I got a place in a hotel, La Chateau Champlain, near Mount Royal and Old Montreal...near Natasha's studio...I took a chance. If we hit it off, I'd get her to show me around the city.

"Novak introduced us and something clicked. I wrapped up my story on the festival and asked Dee to keep Ariel for one more week. I began seeing Natasha every day—ice skating in Angrignon Park, dinner, dancing, movies.

"We'd stay up all night talking. I remember Natasha laughing, 'Now I practice with you English.'

"She smelled of...cinnamon and spoke of herself in the third person. 'Natasha is pulling the pins out of her hair.' 'Natasha travels across Russia on train...Mademoiselle Kaminsky will not fly on airplanes.'

"It turned out both our fathers had been born near Minsk, so right away there was this sense of kinship. Natasha was my *landsmann*, my *shiksa* 'opposite'... Do you understand?

"I told her the truth, that I was drawn to her but that I had some 'history'...that I'd been married three times.

159 ❖

"'Oo, la la, so many times!' she said, 'you frighten me, Nomad.' That was her name for me. The Nomad. 'And tell me, Nomad, what have you learned from three times?'

"To put my family first, that's what I've learned. No screwing around."

"And what is Nomad's truth? What is his truth about Natasha?" she asked.

"That's simple. I want you to visit Ariel and me—spend a week or two in Los Angeles. If you like, if we like, stay longer and meet all my children."

"So Natasha Kaminsky must audition to be your wife?"

"Natasha, that's not what I said. I wasn't proposing."

"What did you say?"

"Try it out...see if you like L.A. See if you like being with us."

"And how do you choose a wife? Three times you chose wrong. What did you look for?'"

"Brains and purple eye shadow," I said, "that's what I was looking for when I met Dee.

"'Now I believe you. But Natasha Kaminsky wears brown eye shadow.'"

"Earth colors are what I'm ready for," I said. "Now brown mascara is fine. So. Tell me your truth."

"'Natasha is a new citizen,'" she said, faking an accent. 'New to Canada, where she meets Noah the ark man and his many children.'"

"Noah the ark man? Is it possible you're looking for a houseboat...or some port, any port, in a storm?"

"'I am caring for you, Noah. If we become friends, I use you, you use me. Trust Natasha. I would not desert you or leave young child like your numero three, Miss Purple Eyeshadow. I'll visit and maybe we'll make bargain.'

"I thought of Ariel. 'Daddy, you say you have to work...' I could imagine Natasha being a companion to her, teaching her to weave. And it wasn't only Ariel...

"Later, we went shopping for Ariel. Making our way through a blizzard, going store to store, I imagined myself walking across Russia. Natasha, I remember, wore blue jeans, red leather boots, a blue sweater and a red scarf. It was -20 degrees and that big mouton coat she had with her—she didn't even wear it.

"While we shopped she told me about her family. Her father, Ivan Kaminsky, had been a tank commander in World War II. He drank, she said, and was violent. In fact, Natasha said all the men in her family drank. Her uncle, 'Vodka Ivan,' was addicted to gambling. 'Ivan the Unpleasant,' she called him. Then there was 'out of work Ivan' (Ivan the Unemployed) and her brother, 'little Ivan,' a student at McGill University. Another brother, Ivan Schmirnoff Kaminsky, she said was a spy for the KGB. All these men had lived in Montreal for about two years.

"What about your mother?" I asked.

"My mother just takes care of my father," she said.

"Natasha worked barefoot at the loom. Her grandmother—also a weaver—had told her wearing shoes is like wearing blinders and that, in any case, it's possible to see with your feet.

"A week after we met she saw me off and made me promise to phone...'every second day for sure.'

"In fact, we talked on the phone every few days for six months. 'Come visit, stay with me...try it out, a week or two,' I'd say, and each time she'd put me off. After four months I sent her $700 to buy tickets.

"'First Natasha must say goodbye, Nomad, and give hugs to close, dear friends.'

"'Natasha, for a little visit?'" I didn't know what she was talking about. What did she mean, 'say goodbye to people'?

"Six months after we met she arrived. She came, by train, with suitcases, cardboard boxes and her walnut loom which filled four packing cases. I ended up renting a U-Haul van and lugging each piece into the house. I wondered if she was as innocent as she seemed.

"'Is that the custom in your country?' I teased her, 'to visit people with everything you own?' I was taken back, almost ready to send her home, but managed to keep my mouth shut. Then, finally, I saw how loving she was with Ariel.

"Ariel took to her immediately. As for me, really, after three marriages I didn't know what I was doing any more.

JUDAISM PERMITS RE-MARRIAGE? Rama writes.

"Not only that, doctor. Rabbis say all past sins are forgiven on the wedding day. Since I'm one of those people whose notion of love is tied in with making a family, it's important for me to be able to do that, to start over each time with a clean slate."

Rama's chalk flies across the board which he then holds for Noah to see.

SIN ABSOLVED. INNOCENCE RESTORED.

"After a couple weeks Natasha fell into the role of Ariel's step mom. With their honey colored hair and blue eyes they even looked like mother and child."

YOU WERE HAPPY, writes the doctor.

"Happy because I saw that Ariel was happy. We were all better off than before. I tried not to think how crazy it was to get married again. But I did love Natasha and she knew it, though after a while she complained all I wanted of her was to be a companion, a step mom, to Ariel.

"I say, *did* love her, but I still do. I still love Shelley and Anna and Dee also. It's true, I hate each of them when the marriages break up, but eventually I come round to feeling connected again, and that feeling, feeling connected, won't go away. I care about the women and I care about my children. I'm not good at hating ex-wives.

"I could slap Holly right now, and beat up on her boyfriend, but that feeling is still there. I'm connected to her.

"What was I saying? Where were we...?

NATASHA MARRIED YOU AND U.S.A., Rama writes.

"Did I say that, doctor? That's funny, that's what I was intending to say.

"Anyway, it didn't take. I mean, how many times can a person be uprooted? Natasha had adapted to Canada and thrived. In L.A. she felt isolated and afraid. And driving frightened her. She refused to learn.

"When she tried to convince me that Ariel needed a little brother or sister, I knew she herself wanted a child. Ariel called Natasha 'Mommy,' and Natasha would teasingly refer to her as 'little big sister,' preparing for the baby to come. This time I became the devoted spouse, nurturer and general factotum. This time, while she complained of being used, of being shackled and unfree, I did all I could to make the marriage work. In a sense I found myself doing for her exactly those things my first and second wives had done for me. Of course I also needed to earn a living and that meant teaching and writing.

YOU WANT A WOMAN WHEN YOU CALL. BUT SHE MUST DISAPPEAR WHEN YOU WRITE. TO WORK, A MARRIAGE NEEDS BALANCE, Rama writes.

"Rama, after three marriages I would have done anything. I didn't want to lose her and, this sounds strange to say, I felt I owed her something.

"Anyway, poor Natasha became pregnant—it was then we got married—and six weeks later she lost the baby. That happened twice, two miscarriages.

"'This L.A. is unhealthy, the air is poisoned,'" she said.

"I couldn't see moving to Montreal and, after the miscarriages, she was sick, homesick...depressed for weeks. We both felt jinxed.

"I asked her if she wanted to try again and she said no.

"We were together for four years and poor Ariel, O God! Losing another mother.

"Anyway, Natasha went back to Montreal...married another Russian émigré and had three children. 'So you see,' she said, 'I was right about L.A.' She still writes, still sends gifts to Ariel.

"You know, a part of me had been looking for someone with a successful career, a woman who was going to pull her own weight, be a full partner.

YOU CHOSE, Rama writes.

"That's true, I chose and I paid the price," Noah answers.

"I don't know about you, doctor," Noah says, "but my mind just chatters on and on. Tell me, does not speaking make a difference in 'mind chatter,' in the talk that goes on in your mind?"

SILENCE IS DONE TO SILENCE THE MIND, Rama writes.

"But if you're silent, you're not praying. Aren't you supposed to pray in some way?'

YOU LOSE SOME, YOU GAIN SOME.

Noah jokes back. "In journalism they say, 'Good quotes up high.' 'Write true story: correct errors or misconceptions.' Those are my mantras."

Noah relaxes. His spirits lift. "You know," he says grinning, "for a moment there I forgot all about my marriages. Doctor, really, I need your help with this story I'm working on. The easy part is interviewing people who claim to know you. What could I do to see things more from your point of view?"

FIRST YOU HAVE TO KNOW ME.

Copying Rama's words into his notebook, Noah underlines *you have to know me* with a yellow, felt-tip pen.

Clearing the chalkboard, Rama writes, THERE ARE MANY DIF-FERENT WAYS OF DESCRIBING A PERSON. I DID NOT WRITE MY OWN STORY. NO ONE IS ALIVE NOW WHO KNOWS ABOUT MY PAST.

"Doctor, there must be someone I can talk to," Noah protests.

I KNEW SOMEONE WHO USED TO COME TO MY CAVE TO WRITE. HE TOLD ME WHEN HE WRITES HE GETS WORDS WHICH HE NEVER HEARD BEFORE. HE WAS A NOVEL WRITER.

"You mean he claimed to be inspired? What was his name?" Noah asks, speaking into his microphone.

GOVIND BALLABH PANT. A HINDI WRITER, writes the doctor.

"Are his books available in this country?"

NOT TRANSLATED INTO ENGLISH.

Noah goes on reading into the recorder what the doctor writes on the chalkboard.

"Does it please you to have someone tell about you?" Noah asks.

IF THEY KNOW, Rama writes.

"How can I write this *Champion of Living* story if there's no documentation, no record of seventy or eighty years of your life and no one to talk to, no one who knows anything about them?"

"*Ssssss.*" Rama's laugh is part noisy snort, part gleeful whisper. The doctor's eyes light up with mischief.

FACT AND FICTION ARE NOT DIFFERENT, he writes.

"Of course they're different," Noah protests.

WHAT IS A FACT NOW WILL BECOME A FICTION AFTER 40 OR 50 YEARS,

"I don't understand."

Using both sides of his 8 x 10 chalkboard, Rama writes:

WHERE I LIVED IN CHILDHOOD WAS A BIG HOUSE WITH A HUGE COURT-YARD. IT WAS A FACT. AFTER 40 YEARS, I WENT THERE AND SAW IT WAS A SMALL HOUSE AND A SMALL COURTYARD. SO THAT FACT IS A FICTION NOW.

"Well, tell me this: are you an ordinary person?"

LOWER, BELOW AN ORDINARY PERSON.

"Do you ever make mistakes?"

IN THE WORLD, EVERYONE MAKES MISTAKES.

"Forgive me," Noah says. "I ask these things with all due respect. I know many people who read this story will be skeptical.

Smiling faintly, Rama shrugs.

"You once wrote *silencing the mind is real silence*. How do you manage to think, how do you go about thinking, if your mind is silent? People I've interviewed, people who claim to know you, say you don't think, at least not in the usual way."

Rama writes, 'I DON'T THINK' DOESN'T MEAN THAT THE MIND IS SHUT OFF. A YOGI THINKS WHEN HE NEEDS TO THINK.

Noah copies, underlines some words and looks across at Rama. His cheeks burn. He might at least have brought the man some flowers or a bowl of fruit. In India, he knows, it is customary to bring offerings when one visits women, children, physicians and kings.

Imagine if Rama were a master of the sort one sees in cartoons—sitting cross-legged on a mountain top. And what if he, Noah, were the seeker come at last into the presence of a being who could answer any question, fulfill any wish?

Noah can have anything he wants: Peace of mind. Eternal life. Fame and fortune.

"What can I do for you?" asks the wise one.

"I want my family intact. Bring her back, O silent one. Bring back Holly and my son."

17

Marriage #5
Man Files to Divorce Himself

Mt. Chakra, The Santa Cruz Mountains

3:00 P.M.

MARRIAGE FIVE?

The doctor hasn't finished with him yet. Rama's chalk stick moves quickly on the little board.

WHO LEFT WHOM?

"Isn't this where I came in? You know. Holly left."

WHY?

He shrugs thinking of Holly and their long-distance marriage, how one or both of them left home for weeks at a time. The "Bad Girl" soap star and the sixty-hour-a-week writer-teacher. The fights, quarrels. Their sleeping together. Their not sleeping together. Their inability to talk to one another. Sex. And what passed for sex.

"I don't know," he says. He's hurting. He's had enough.

SHE FOUND YOU BORING. SHE WANTS FUN, writes the doctor.

"What do you mean *boring?*" He feels the blood drain from his heart. "Who asked you, anyway?" He wonders how he'll get through the next twenty-four hours. He punches himself—lightly—in the stomach and wonders how he's ever going to eat again with no appetite and a mouth like dried turkey feathers. Boring? I go to Mt. Chakra to see the Champion of Living, and he says I'm boring.

SITUATION SUGGESTS HOLLY WILL REMAIN WITH THIS NEW MAN, Rama writes.

Noah blinks. His mind stops. His heart and breathing stop.

DIFFERENCE IN AGES?

"Thh-thirteen years," stammers the husband. I'm 47. Sssh-she's 34."

NOT SO MUCH.

"She's actually older. She looks 34, and so she lies about her age and just now, with you, I was doing what she asked me to do. I'm supporting her by lying about her age. I'm just another married fool being led around by the nose.

"Am I a boring person?" he asks. He knows the answer. His work comes first. Not so. Women come first. Sex comes first. Love and the family come first because he believes he needs a family to be happy. When does his work come first? When he's secure. When he's in a relationship that feels settled. But he never puts in enough effort. It takes time to make a family work and he needs the time to write.

He loved Holly, Ariel, and his hyperactive son, but he also loved having them out of the way. *Out of the way* meant out of the house when he was working at home. No matter how quiet they were, their very presence—tiptoeing around, playing music, however softly—was a distraction.

Now that they were gone, Noah's *Champion of Living* story seemed meaningless. Worse, he found he was bored with himself. Bored? Bored.

He's guilty, guilty as charged. He used his family as a springboard to write.

If it were possible for a man to leave himself, Noah would now leave. Another divorce, that's what he wants. He imagines the headlines at a supermarket checkout counter:

Much-Married Man Divorces Himself

SAN FRANCISCO, CA. Journalist Noah Newmark, 47, today became the first person in history to divorce himself...

What follows is a copy of the 'Dear John' letter the feature writer left himself.

Noah Newmark, I've had enough.
We're incompatible. I want out of this relationship.
I want out of my skin. Goodbye

Rama sips tea and waits for Noah to continue.

Noah nods. He imagines a temple, a synagogue-on-wheels. Belonging to a Reformed congregation, the synagogue, its engine running, spewing exhaust, is shaped like an airport bus. Looking in from the outside, he sees a bride and groom. Holly is the bride. She's standing under a *chuppa*, a canopy of white silk. He's unable to identify the groom.

One side of the bus is filled with all the people he has left or divorced. The other side is filled with all the people who have left or divorced him. Shabby, Chagall-like *klezmorim* are playing violins. Meanwhile, sitting in the driver's seat, an elderly rabbi busies himself making change.

"Sorry," he says, "no transfers."

Noah sees his mother, dead for over thirty years. His mother's mother. His father's father. His father's mother.

"There I go again, blaming people for being dead," he says to his mother. "Mom, I'm sorry. God forgive me, I never even said *Kaddish* for you."

"When Sholom Aleichem's mother died, she had six sons to say *Kaddish* after her," says his mother.

"Mom, I'm sorry. I just want you to know I still mourn. My whole life I mourned for you."

"There's a Jewish saying: *When a son gets married, he divorces his mother*, she answers. "Four times you divorced me, Noah. Such a son. What am I to think?"

"Mom, could you forgive me? Look, I've even divorced myself, for Godsake!"

"Noah, you're still my son. Of course I forgive you."

When at last the exhaust fumes lift, he sees his very much alive stepbrothers, his half brother, his other wives—a few on one side of the bus, a few on the other—and all their relatives, all those families which once had been his families. Married or not to the beautiful pride and joy of those families, Noah suddenly hungers, as he had never hungered before, to be a part of their households.

Rama raps on his chalkboard.

"Huh?" says the writer, reaching for his notebook. "I'm sorry, doctor, this will just take a moment," he mumbles.

He speedwrites:

> What do you call a person who belongs, or longs to belong, simultaneously to five families? Divorced, one rants against one's former spouse. Eventually one gets over the ranting. What I find I haven't gotten over, is a hunger for something larger, a hunger for the families themselves.

Noah grieves for his in-laws, his lost mothers-in-law, his lost fathers-in-law, the nieces and nephews, the teasing, usually loving sisters-in-law, the teasing, but less loving brothers-in-law. He longs for the celebrations, the weddings, the births, the birthdays, even the funerals of his in-laws, and of course the food, tables groaning under the weight of turkeys—food for sixty, ninety, a hundred people. The side dishes, the matzo ball soup, the antipasto, the gravy, the casseroles, the fresh green salads, loaves of rye bread and challah, the bowls of fruit, desserts, O strawberry shortcake, O homebaked apple pie with ice cream, fragrance of fresh ground coffee, vodka, wine and beer.

His chest heaves as he sees the women he dumped and those who dumped him. Teammates and coaches from teams he played on and then quit. Teammates and managers from teams he played on who quit on him.

And the children who are no longer with him: Joey, Jim and Carol. The children he lost through his own foolishness. Thank God, thank God he got to raise Ariel!

He reaches for a handkerchief.

ENOUGH ALREADY, Rama writes.

"Are you reading my mind? What do you know about what goes on in my head?" Noah snaps. Jesus Christ, he thinks. What is it with this guy? How much shit is he going to unload on me? How much more can I take?

The silent one shakes his head. *No, no.* The words *don't misunderstand* sound in Noah's head. They come into his mind without the doctor having to write or speak them.

DIFFERENT NATURES, the doctor writes.

"'Different natures,'" the writer repeats. "So I'm not boring." Noah takes a long, slow breath. "It's true, Holly and I are different natures. Of all my wives, if I have an opposite, she's my opposite. You're right. But that was part of her appeal. And maybe that's what she liked about me, that I was so unlike her. Does that make sense? Anyway, after four tries at compatibility, with Holly I thought I'd go the other way."

The doctor isn't finished with him. WHY DO THEY LEAVE YOU? Silent, shamed. Can't think of a damn thing to say. Why did I come to him? What possessed me? This yogi-physician, this walking confession box. What's in it for him? Why should he care? How would a 101-year-old celibate know anything about why women leave?

"I don't know why."

BECAUSE THEY WANT YOU, NOT WORDS. YOU LIVE IN YOUR HEAD. YOU LIVE THROUGH LANGUAGE. THAT DOESN'T EXCITE THEM.

"You mean I'm too self-absorbed, don't you? That I live in an abstract world, that I translate everything that goes on in my life into words, that I write all the time, even when I'm desperate?"

HOLLY WAS AFRAID TO TELL YOU SHE DOESN'T WANT TO REMAIN MARRIED. IT WAS IN HER MIND FOR A LONG TIME. SHE WAS WAITING FOR THE RIGHT MOMENT.

"What? How do you know?" says Noah.

Flashback to Holly saying: "All you care about is your work."

And his reply: "That's not true. Your happiness is more important to me than anything. I can't work well unless I know you're happy."

"That's why you want Joey and me happy. So your conscience can be clear and you can work."

"Well, I guess so. But what about you, Holly?"

"I'd like to see you happy. I'd like for both of our consciences to be clear."

DO YOU ACCEPT THAT MARRIAGE MAY BE OVER? writes the doctor.

"Hell no, I can't accept that the marriage is over." Noah pauses. Reconsiders. The last shall be first, the first shall be last, he thinks. Maybe. Okay. If he's prepared to give Holly up, it's just possible he can win her back. But first he has to be willing to give her up. Can he honestly say he's willing to let her go? Let her go. No, yes, no... Noah nearly chokes getting the word out. At last he says, "Yes."

Is Rama still insisting that the marriage is over? Maybe it's somehow personal and the physician disliked Holly from the day he saw her. Maybe he disapproves of TV daytime "Bad Girl" soap stars, especially those who wear mink coats to yoga classes. Well, she only did that once. At 6 A.M. it's generally cold at Mt. Chakra.

THEN IT WILL BE EASY, the doctor writes.

"That I accept that it's over makes it easy? What will be easy? Knowing Holly and Joey are with another man? Charlie Schumacher, for example, replacing me, the old husband? Holly in bed with Charlie right now watching television? Doctor, what do you know about easy ?"

Noah knows what's coming next. He needs some resolution. He's going to have to go and see her. Fly to New York and try to hunt her down.

Looking at Rama, Noah sees a mirror-image of himself: ruddy cheeks, longish beard, furrowed brow, steel-rimmed spectacles.

What's he up to?

Noah licks his lips. Inhales slowly.

Again he has the sensation that what thoughts arise in his mind, arise also in the doctor's. That his mind and the doctor's are, in some essential way, one, and that inside of his skull is a chalkboard receiving Rama's messages directly.

SHE DID NOT SAY WHETHER SHE IS LEAVING YOU, WHETHER SHE WILL COME BACK OR WANTS TO STAY.

His dry lips and tongue move against his teeth. He reads the chalkboard to see if it corroborates what he already thinks.

YOU MAY HAVE TO SEE HER TO ACCEPT IT.

Noah protests. "Don't you understand? I have a deadline on the *Champion of Living* story. I'm not sure I want to see her."

IF SHE DOESN'T WANT TO STAY MARRIED THEN YOU CAN'T FORCE HER. BUT YOU HAVE TO GET SOME CLEAR ANSWER. IF YOU DON'T GO, THEN THINGS WILL REMAIN SUSPENDED.

The door to the doctor's living room opens and Noah, just as it closes, catches sight of men and women waiting their turn. Some, unlike Noah, have come bearing gifts, a bouquet of flowers, a bowl of fruit.

Standing, Rama makes his way to an umbrella holder. Raising a whip-like cluster of blue-green feathers, he swats the writer on the head.

Noah, taking this as a signal the interview is over, puts down his notebook and shuts off the cassette player.

"How can I thank you?" Noah pauses, expecting the physician to gesture somehow with his hand or maybe write on his chalkboard. Closing his briefcase, he's about to stand when he hears a sudden *Swoosh.*

THWACK!

Vibrating, the room spins and enlarges.

"Goddamn..." he hears someone say. And again, "God" (*Thwack!* he has the sensation of his brains being swooshed), "Damn" (*Woosh!* he's outside his body, attentive, watchful), "Sonofabitch!" (he's limitless, a newborn child). *Swoosh!*

Recoiling, Noah opens his eyes to see the doctor, peacock feathers in hand, smiling as if in greeting.

Rama's mouth opens, "*ssss...sssss...*" he laughs and reaches for his chalkboard. PEACE, he writes. ENOUGH.

18

San Francisco
International Airport

Overnight bag in one hand, notebook in the other, Noah boards Bi-Coastal Airline Flight 007, the Redeye Special. He speedwrites:

Jalopy aircraft from the 1970s with yesteryear Muzak. A tug. Then another tug. We're still on the ground. Our plane is being towed backwards to the runway. Passengers lulled by piped-in strains of two-step, tootsie roll *September Song. It's a long long time between May and December...*

Redhead, redeye flight attendant distributes stereo headsets. Seeing the wintry woman next to me plug in and turn to the Yesterday Once More ('C'etait hier') channel, she laughs. 'Nostalgia isn't what it used to be, is it?' she says. Expecting to hear 1940s and '50s *schmaltz*, my aging seat companion gets the Kinks singing *You Really Got Me* and James Brown's upbeat *I Feel Good...I Got You*. The wit and wisdom of Audio Entertainment. Audio voyeur, I turn on the same channel. Aretha Franklin comes on with *Until You Come Back To Me*. Then it's Elvis' turn: *That's When Your Heartaches Begin*. Elvis knew. The king knew.

Moments before take-off, Noah re-reads Rama's last words to him: HOPE IS LIFE. IT'S ALL A GAME. FALSE EXPECTATION IS THE CAUSE OF "BROKEN HEART." NOTHING IS PERMANENT. BUT WE ARE LOOKING FOR PERMANENCE.

He struggles to undo his seatbelt, to stand and run for the nearest exit. "Elvis! Help! Let me out of here!"

Then, stoically, he settles back into his seat and writes:

> After all the preliminaries, what a bitch if the plane crashes, and I don't get to finish...

Once, while researching a story on the Queen Charlotte Islands, he had taken off in a storm. Freezing rain had begun pouring into the cabin. "Loose rivets," explained the flight attendant holding a newspaper over her head. "Vancouver Island Airway. You know our motto? *If your time is up, it doesn't matter what you're flying.*"

Noah shuts his eyes trying to remember where he heard the line, *We are such stuff as dreams are made of, and our little life is rounded with a sleep.* Elvis Presley. Elvis Presley, he decides, in that song *That's When Your Heartaches Begin.*

When the "No Smoking" and "Fasten Your Seatbelt" signs go off, he orders a martini. Adjusting the stereo headset, switching to CHANNEL 3, he hears a familiar voice.

"...My fiancé is going to buy me new boobs for a wedding present. You know, the kind that stand up on their own. We're going to Utah to get it done. Boobs are cheaper there. Oh, Noah, did I tell you? I'm getting married again."

He reaches for his pen.

"Is that you, Dolores?" he asks, turning up the volume.

She doesn't answer. She just goes right on talking.

"It used to be that your fiancé bought you gifts. Well, I guess boobs are gifts. I think so."

He writes:

Fiancé buys his bride-to-be customized boobies.
Is this wedding gift more for the groom than for
the bride? Is this the gift that goes on giving?

"God bless you, Dolores. I hope he's good to you," Noah
says, switching channels.

CHANNEL 2. "I remember when I went into labor with Jimmy
and Noah wouldn't acknowledge it."

"I was working on an article," Noah says aloud. "I had a
deadline. Is that you, is that really you, Anna? How are you, darling?"

Anna's silent.

Grimacing as if to reassure him, his seat companion stands
and reaches for her overnight bag. Noah helps her with the bag
and nods as she moves to the rear of the plane.

Anna continues with her story.

"Do you know what he said to me? 'You're not,' he said, 'you
only think you're in labor.'

"I said, 'But Noah, I'm having contractions. I know what I'm
feeling.'

"And Noah, the bastard, said, 'Well, I'll do the *I Ching*.'

"'What are you going to ask?' I said.

"'If it's time to go to the hospital,' he said.

"What a marriage! What a marriage!" Anna cries. "I can't
believe what I put up with."

"I remember you used to say I was one of a kind," Noah
offers, but she doesn't answer. He can hear Anna, but she can't
hear him.

CHANNEL 1. Ready for anything, Noah changes channels again.
He overhears Shelley Levine, his first wife, confiding in her therapist.

"Noah was looking for a retro-woman, someone to do the laundry and play second fiddle. But I wanted a career. I wanted to earn money. Noah, in his mind, was the main event. I felt swallowed up in his identity. I felt I'd end up like my mother."

"Shelley, is that you? That's not like you. You sound pissed..."

"He was a man of the world, I thought. For me he was Charles Boyer. He was the Humphrey Bogart of sex. I never told him this and he never confided in me either. We never confided much in each other. Not then we didn't. Now we do.

"Well, it's his own fault. I tried. You know, Henry Ford was right: *Stick to the first model,* he said, and he wasn't talking about cars."

CHANNEL 4. "...I'm a new woman," says his fourth wife. "In Russian theater there are two Natashas. One is prim and proper with pins in her hair, a sort of schoolmarm.

"Now Natasha is leading lady. Friends and admirers give teas and dinners in her honor. Natasha pulling the pins out of her hair. I am beautiful woman men desire. Also, I'm not so round any more."

"Natasha, Natasha!" he calls, but it's another one-way conversation.

CHANNEL 5. "...You know what I like about afternoon soaps?" Holly asks. "That the plots have no beginning and no end and that there are lots of petty, little crises. And then there's this big climax on Friday to hold peoples' attention until Monday.

"That suits my temperament. I like clichés. My professional life, playing Penelope, is predicated on clichés. Clichés are the one thing in my life I can count on. Clichés provide security. They're reassuring. Just think about it. Happy beginnings are re-assuring. Happy endings are reassuring.

"Of course we know in real life there are no happy endings. You're lucky to get a happy middle. You're lucky to get a happy anything. Am I right? Oh, sorry. Charlie's here. I gotta go."

"Holly, Holly..." he cries.

There's a clicking noise. Then he hears a buzzing, a faint but familiar "*Pssst*," the sound Rama uses when he wants to get someone's attention.

"Doctor? Doctor, is that you?"

At last, pulling off the headset, he unplugs the earphones.

Married, faithful to Holly for so many years, he reflects on his state. "*De-wedded*," he speedwrites. The word *un-wedded* follows. Then the words *un-bedded, un-paired, de-paired, in despair, un-cemented, dis-united, de-married, horror* and *loss* pour onto the page.

"What can you do with a man who goes around consoling himself with language? Is it possible for a man to be more at home with language than with women?"

"Perhaps I like it like this," he scribbles.

"Will you always love me?" Holly had asked on their honeymoon. "What would make you not love me?"

"If you went off to some awards ceremony and had an affair, or lied to me about something important, or told a whole lot of little lies," he answered.

"Would you love me if I never did anything else with my life, if I got old in soaps?"

"Holly, that's a silly question. You know the answer to that."

He remembers reaching for Holly's hand on the honeymoon flight—to Honolulu. "I hope you don't mind flying," he'd asked.

"I'm not afraid, if that's what you mean. I'm too well-groomed to die."

Laughing, tears in his eyes, Noah reached into his pocket for the wedding gift, diamond earrings from Cartier. The journalist launched into his fifth marriage as he had launched into his first, second, third and fourth, the word *Amor* on his lips.

His skin shivers now with warmth as he recalls how Holly had, on their honeymoon, dipped a feather applicator into what was, apparently, an edible powder. Flicking it lightly across Noah's body...

What was that scent?

He recalls her first letter, written after he interviewed her for *Fanfare Magazine*. Enclosing a signed photo and ticket stub for a movie she'd just seen, *Raiders of the Lost Ark* ("it's worth seeing more than once"), she began by praising his feature:

> Dear Noah,
>
> I hope you don't mind my calling you 'Noah'?
>
> I just got my copy of *Fanfare* and I'm writing to say how pleased I am...Friends tell me it's rare for a journalist to respect the person he's writing about and actually come up with something moving and intelligent that doesn't exploit the celebrity—though I'm hardly a celebrity at this point in my career. But then I'm not exactly a "soap slick ingénue" either...

Writing with a felt tip pen on one side of the page, she continued onto the other:

> Thank you for catching the true Holly Hollander. Your understanding me makes me feel I could do the same with you—understand you, I mean. I feel very fortunate. Friends in the show are always getting upset about how journalists portray them.
>
> I'm told the pattern is to run three friendly pieces on a celebrity and then a fourth that tears the person into little pieces. Journalists build people up and then

they shoot them down. I've got something to look forward to, right?

Can you read my god-awful handwriting? I could BLOCK PRINT, but it tends to make the content rigid and predictable. So here it is. Some say it's illegible—completely, utterly indecipherable. Of course I tend to disagree. Not that I don't sometimes have problems making it out myself. However, I secretly feel that those who find my handwriting wholly impossible to understand must find me impossible to understand. And, as an actress, I suppose, that's not necessarily a bad thing. Cause I know how seductive that can be.

The fire is purring in my living room and Elton John is singing *Butterflies Are Free To Fly*. It's approaching midnight and it's been a long day.

My life. My work. They are interchangeable. Always. Healthy? I don't really know, really care. I just feel it's part of being. Just being. At least for me. Anyway, I'm working a lot, as you know, shooting the new season. It's arduous, superficial, rarely free, financially generous and a weird place to be. I hate Planet Hollywood.

Tell me a little about yourself. You know so much about me. Were you always a writer? Do you remember the first time you said out loud to someone, 'I am a writer?' I'd be interested in your answer.

Ciao,
Holly

P.S. I know it's a cliché, but I've never been moved to write a letter like this before.

CHANNEL 0. Putting the headset back on, Noah once more switches channels. "Mom," he says, recognizing her voice, "is that you?" He imagines his mother as he knew her, noshing, listening to soap opera and talking at the same time on the phone to Ida, her friend. Then his nostrils fill with the smell, schmaltz, chicken fat, smeared on Jewish rye bread. And another smell, Chesterfield cigarettes.

"I tell you, things aren't going so good for Noah. He's had all these marriages. Really, Ida, do you think it has to do with my dying like that?" he hears his mother say. "I'm still trying to figure it out. Doesn't he know all that love I gave him is still inside him? I feel so guilty," she says. He hears her voice in the center of his own throat. "Even for dying, I feel guilty."

Removing the headset, Noah reaches for his martini.

At 10 A.M., on Boxing Day, that's appropriate, he thought, he'll call Sarah Speir, his lawyer. Silver, Stiletto, Hartless & Speir. *Dissolution a specialty.* New York's best with offices in California. He's been through it before. He has to think ahead. Just in case. One day soon, if all else fails, he'll be The Defendant and Holly will be paying some pit bull to be versus him. After meeting with Sarah Speir, he'll phone the bank. See if he can afford another divorce. He's already sent on a telegram care of TV actress JoBeth Winter, Holly's friend: "Dearest Holly. Arriving in New York Christmas Eve. Will phone. Love you."

He'll stand on his head, move to the East Coast, do anything in his power to stay with her. His prayer? That Dr. Rama is wrong. That he'll return from this trip with Holly and Joey. On the other hand...

Dreams

4:26 A.M.– CHRISTMAS EVE

"In sleep, it is not the man who sins—but his dream."
            —Jewish saying

DREAM I

Thirty-five thousand feet over snow-struck Omaha, Nebraska, the plane kept aloft in part by the faith of its passengers, their confident belief that they will arrive at their destination, he dreams of the movie *Annie Hall* and the sequence where Woody Allen tries to win back Diane Keaton—flies to California to see her—and convince the love of his life to return to New York. All she says is, "Let's be friends." Friendship, *schmendship*. Noah is not an evolved yogi. He's not an evolved anything. He is a de-wedded, de-bedded, uxorious feature writer. All of a sudden, wishing her death, he decides he'd like to see Holly launched on a leaky, twice-used, fire-breathing, giant rubber prophylactic, a dong-shaped space capsule to the moon. Boom! But God, he decides, no longer wishing for her death, I love her. The truth is, I want her back.

DREAM 2

Noah is climbing a steep, ice-slick, tree-covered hill. The higher he gets, the more clearly he hears Holly's voice warning him off, "Stop climbing. You're not ready." But he's drawn to her like a heat-seeking missile. For a moment—myopically—he sees Holly just inches away. He sees her eyes and nothing else. Then he's able to see her hairline and forehead and nothing else. The two of them engage in a peaceable exchange without once looking at one another.

Noah thinks of Joy (AKA Sandra Rothchild) who, before he left Mt. Chakra, had put her heavy arm around his neck and hugged him.

About to board the airport bus, moved by the gesture, he had turned and kissed her lightly on the cheek.

"A lawyer without makeup, a master-at-arms, but you can't

hide it, Joy, you're very attractive," Noah said.

"Spoken like my own brother," she laughed.

"I know what's in your heart and I wish you well," she says. "You know, you're not alone."

"I know. I know."

"Look, Noah, there are no guarantees. Maybe Holly will be in New York and maybe she won't. But you go as a new person and, if your wife is there, share heart to heart without judging her or yourself. And if you go and she's not there, that's alright too. The thing is to set aside any preordained conclusions you may have about Holly. At the same time, do what you can to help Holly to set aside her preconceptions. If you can do that, you will begin to see with compassion. Going to New York, seeing your wife, is meditation.

"That's what he teaches, *consciousness in action*."

"Inaction? I'm for action, not inaction," Noah laughed.

"You know what I'm saying."

"Well, what good is it, Joy? Is the loss of the people we love most in life, a tool of some kind? Is everything that happens, a 'tool for growth'? I like my attachments."

"If all the time you're with a person, Noah, you're worrying they're going to walk out on you or get more famous or die or something, you're not free. You said it yourself: *Everything is alive and life is change. Every moment all things change.* But the doctor says, WHEN THE THORN OF ATTACHMENT IS PULLED OUT, THERE IS PEACE IN THE HEART.

"You know, it's not Holly who's causing you pain, but your attachment to her."

"Excuse me, but this is too airy, Joy, though I suppose what you're saying is that where there's no attachment, there's no pain."

"You got it."

"What I don't got, Joy, is how to get rid of the attachment."

"Noah, when you write an article, doesn't the story sometimes unfold by itself?"

"Yeah, in the really good features it does, the ones I'm proud of."

"That's possible because in the features you're proud of, you somehow managed to let go of your need for control. You go with what unfolds.

"You've been blessed. Don't you see? You have two obsessions: writing and women. Most people never find anything they're committed to like that. You're lucky. If you can work it out with Holly, that's also a blessing. And if you don't work it out, you'll have more time for your other obsession. Tell me, if you don't work it out, will you be dopey enough to complain you have too much freedom? Either way you will find peace because either way you're blessed."

"Thanks, Joy. God, my God. How can I lose?"

19

Leap of Faith

New York City

Suddenly dropping 300 feet, the Bi-Coastal 747 pitches and rolls, levels out and begins regaining altitude. Approaching JFK Airport, the plane seems to accelerate and then slow down as the cabin lights blink on and off. Rattling and vibrating, the plane makes its way to the top of a slowly spiraling funnel, a constellation of lights circling the City.

"Well, folks," the pilot's voice comes crackling into the cabin, "I don't need to tell you we're experiencing a little weather.

"Those of you with window seats can see by the lights that we're at the top of a stack of planes. We're waiting for clearance to land, but that looks like forty-five minutes.

"For your safety...'Fasten Your Seat Belt' signs have been turned on. We're experiencing...expect to encounter new turbulence as we...Wup! Wup!

"We just have to wait our turn."

Noah winces as his ears pop.

"Frankly, I've never seen it this bad. Shit. My God, where did...did you see that?" demands the pilot, dropping the milk and cookies voice.

Two flight attendants, turning to exchange glances, race to the cockpit. Seconds later the cabin vibrates with a much-amplified hiss, "For Godsake, you guys..."

The intercom clicks off.

"This isn't my flight. I'm not supposed to be on this plane," protests a small, white-haired woman across the aisle from Noah. "Have you flown a lot...aren't you frightened...is this normal?" she asks, peering at him through rimless bifocals.

"We'll be alright," Noah says, sounding confident. "And the plane's almost empty. That's a good thing. They should have plenty of fuel..."

"I would have thought...Christmas Eve...there'd be more people," she whines.

"Flying these days you never know what to expect," says her seat mate, a red-faced man in a dark, pin-striped suit.

"I almost never fly. This morning...I...to cancel because of a dream I had. The plane crashed," she groans. "'You're just being foolish, Grandma.' That's what she said, my daughter-in-law laughed at me."

"Well, you're a brave woman to fly after that," says her seat mate, mopping his brow. "As they say, we're all hostages when the wheels go up."

"There's another world out there even if we can't see it," says the woman, reaching for a vial of pills.

"I agree," Noah says, "but tell me, do you believe everything in our life is arranged in advance?"

"I believe in divine providence," says the woman, licking green and yellow pellets from the flat of her hand. "Without that I think I'd go insane. It's lack of faith makes people crazy. Without God the world would be a maze without a clue."

"Do you believe?"

"Yes, but I'm not sure God always has our best interests at heart," Noah says.

"The Bible tells us otherwise. God knows and cares about every creature," says the woman.

"That may be, but...my father tells a story..."

The woman turns to her seat mate.

"I'm sorry. I thought I saw something...Go on," she says, her eyes again on Noah.

"A rabbi became heartsick over all the suffering and injustice in the world. At last he decided to organize a tribunal and put God on trial."

The woman gasps.

"As my father tells it, the rabbi rounded up twelve men, twelve judges, and summoned God Himself to appear on the witness stand.

"For three weeks these people presented charges and, at the same time, tried to defend God. They fasted and prayed, they consulted the Torah and the Talmud. They argued among themselves. They called in expert witnesses. They did everything in their power to come up with a fair verdict.

"Finally, they reached a unanimous decision."

"How did they find God?" says the businessman, leaning forward.

"Guilty, sir."

"Guilty? Guilty of what?" demands the businessman.

"Guilty of creating Evil in the first place and then turning it loose in the world. What did He want to do that for? Further, the tribunal found God guilty of making no effort to provide for people who others had abandoned, innocent people who, through no fault of their own, were left to die in the street."

"I want to see my grandchildren...I've heard enough blasphemy.

"I don't feel very well," she goes on.

"Ahem, this is Cap'n Rickenbacker. Sorry to alarm you, folks. But really, we've handled emer...incidents like this before. Happens more often than you know. It looks like the worst is over. Glad to have you on board. Nothing to be concerned about."

Her lips parting, the white-haired woman sinks into her seat.

"I'm sorry, m'am," Noah apologizes. Here, I've got this unopened Canada Dry," he offers.

"Hmm, yes," the woman nods.

"Thank you, young man."

"Forty-seven isn't so young," Noah teases.

"My goodness, you certainly fooled me!" Revived, the woman shakes her head. "It's gotten so it's impossible to guess peoples' ages. I'm 79," she says brightly.

"Now I'm surprised. I would have guessed you were in your late 60s at the most."

"Well, that's very kind of you," she says. "My name is Grace Marshall and you're...?

"Noah Newmark."

"Scotch, soda, martinis..." says a tall, dark-haired flight attendant appearing in the aisle.

"I'll have a martini," says Noah, his eyes glassy.

"And you, m'am?"

The woman hesitates.

"Oh, I might as well too," she says at last.

"My treat," says Noah pulling out his wallet. "And, hey, it's Christmas...I'll buy drinks for everyone on the plane."

"No, no, they're complimentary," says the flight attendant. "In fact, if you like, you can have two."

"Well, thank you. And happy holidays, Grace," he says, holding up the plastic cup. "You said you're going to see your grandchildren..."

Hitting an air pocket, the plane drops for a second.

"Oh, my God!" she cries.

"Young man, tell me the truth. Aren't you afraid?" she asks, spilling half her drink.

"No, I'm not afraid of dying, but I do want to be around for my kids. I can't help feeling...unfinished in some ways...But most of all," Noah says, setting down his drink, "most of all I'd like to see how my kids turn out."

"How many do you have?"

"Four."

"You're a lucky man. How old are they?"

Pulling photos out of an envelope, Noah says, "This is Joey, my youngest. He's eight. And this is Ariel, she's 19. Jim is 28; and this is Carol, 26.

"I'm proud of them, though I haven't been the best of fathers."

"You've been married more than once I suppose..." A look of disapproval on her face, the woman turns back to what remains of her martini.

"I'm guilty...All my life I knew what needed to be done. I just didn't do it."

"It's never too late," she says, relenting. "Maybe you've learned something." She bites her lip. *Many shall run to and fro, and knowledge shall be increased.* Do you know the Bible?" she asks, beckoning for another martini.

Noah nods.

"You've been married..." Grace hesitates.

"Five times."

"Oh, my God!" she says, crossing herself.

"Should I ring...Are you feeling ill...?"

"I'm Catholic."

"M'am, it's late in the game, but you're right. Crazy as it may sound, I'm against divorce too. Just don't ask me how that jibes..."

"May I ask you something? Were they awful, your marriages?"

"Really, they weren't so bad. Certainly not awful...looking back on them...they were happy marriages much of the time. I heard a woman say once she had three successful marriages, and I could say the same. I've come to believe if something ends, it doesn't necessarily mean it was a mistake."

"Would you do it again?" the woman asks, wrinkling her brow.

"If you mean do I have regrets, the answer's no. How could I? I mean, those marriages did produce four wonderful children. On the other hand, if you're asking would I do it, marry again, no, I wouldn't."

"You made mistakes."

"Of course I made mistakes. I did crazy things but...I also tried."

"I believe you, Mr. Newmark," she says, sipping from her drink. Pausing, she goes on. "I hear you saying you're thankful."

"Hail Mary," shouts the woman, looking to the window, "they've come! The angels have come for us!"

One hand on his seatback, steadying himself, Noah peers into the night sky.

"I'm sorry, Mrs. Marshall, I don't..."

"Over there," she says, "half way out on the wing."

He sees nothing, swirling snow and mist.

"Oh, Grace, it's just an illusion. A reflection of the plane's lights..."

Still, spurred by Grace's suggestion, about to turn back to his seat, he sees a glow. Then a second, silvery-white, a third, and a fourth...

"There...yes, I see five," he says. "They're wearing wedding gowns."

Arms around one another's waist, the five, the movements of one synchronized with the movements of the others, kick like dancers in a Broadway show.

One-step, two-step, heel and toe. Clog dance, tap-dance, bunny hop, cakewalk, can-can, Castlewalk, Charleston, cha-cha-cha.

Holding hands, the women skip and hop.

"We're about to crash, aren't we?"

"No, m'am, I don't think so. Those are my wives."

"Funny, now I don't see anything," says Grace, turning to the businessman.

Noah waves.

"I still care about you." He mouths the words, praying the women can read his lips. "Shelley, you're my best friend. And Anna, I always knew you were an angel. And Dee, Dee darling, I still dream about you. And Natasha, you too, I care about you and I love your tapestries...O, my sweethearts!" But he can see from their faces they can't make out a word he's saying.

Phantoms. Phantoms in their wedding gowns. A pentagon of wives.

He puts down the martini.

Lights flash on and off.

An overhead luggage bin opens. Hats, a brief case and a pillow fly through the cabin.

Her eyes shut, head back, mouth moving, Grace fingers her rosary. "Hail Mary..."

"Stay in your seats, folks. Keep your seat belts fastened...this landing..." says the pilot, "We're...we're losing power. Flight attendents," he calls.

Regaining power, the plane suddenly banks and begins to climb.

"We survived another one," says the businessman. "But stay tuned, there's more to come."

Gazing into his half-filled martini glass, Noah sees the reflection of two German Messerschmitts.

"Keep your seatbelts fastened," says the pilot. "I'm sorry, but it appears we're about to come under attack. You know how it is...when you least expect it. It's those attorneys you've been hearing about on the news. Macho Family Law Specialists who've been buying vintage World War I and World War II fighters to attack civilian planes.

"Here they come. It's Christmas Eve for Godsake!"

"Noah, would you mind passing me that copy of the *Times*?" says Mrs. Marshall.

"Uh, huh." Looking up from his martini, Noah obliges.

"...I'm just looking over our passenger list." The pilot pauses. "Ah, Noah...Newmark. I know that name. Yeah, you were in the Air Force, weren't you, buddy? Remember Captain Eddie Rickenbacker, your old gunnery instructor? I want you to take that 50 mm weapon over the wing. That's it, Noah. Just put on those headphones and flak jacket."

Pursued by a 1942 Messerschmitt with the image of a paterfamilias and the words *Egocentric male without a clue* on its wings, Rickenbacker puts the 747 into a dive.

Guns blazing, moving at full throttle, the Messerschmitt closes in on the 747.

"Now, let's see if you learned anything, Noah. Fire away!"

The words *Egocentric male in his sights*, Noah squeezes the trigger.

BLAP BLAP BLAP.

He watches as the German fighter, trailing gas and smoke, bursts into flames.

Briefly silhouetted against the moon, a second Messerschmitt, guns spitting fire, attacks the old passenger jet. Looking through his gunsight, Noah makes out four names on the plane's fuselage.

Silver, Stiletto, Hartless & Speir.

"My own lawyers!" he cries, pulling the trigger.

BLAP BLAP BLAP.

The plane's wing carrying the SS law firm's motto, *Specializing in Family Breakup and False Expectations since 1942*, breaks off from the Messerschmitt. Sarah Speir and the other Family Law specialists bail out. Their chutes open.

Going into a tailspin, falling to earth, the vintage war plane trails attaché cases, Child Custody documents and Support orders. The night sky fills with Mutual Release Agreements, Income and Expense declarations, Notices of Judgment...

BOOM BOOM BOOM. Silver, Stiletto's Messerschmitt explodes.

"I represent your wife, Mr. Newmark," says Sarah Spier, dangling from her parachute, briefcase in hand. "We're suing, you s.o.b., your wife is suing for divorce."

"Damn rough weather, eh?" says the businessman.

Buckled into his aisle seat, right arm braced against the seat in front of him, preparing to lead Mrs. Marshall to the nearest exit, Noah is thrown violently forward and back.

Hitting an air pocket, the plane dips, tilts to one side, and a tall brunette falls into Noah's lap. It's the leggy flight attendant.

"It's my ankle. Oh, it hurts," she cries, her eyes wide, her face white.

"I'm so embarrassed. It's crazy. I'm just filling in for someone..."

"No, damnit, no!" Noah speaks to the stirring in his groin. "It's just a fucking reflex. It doesn't mean anything," he reminds himself.

"I'm not sure I can walk."

"Let's try," Noah says, helping her to her feet.

"I think I'll do better without my shoes," she says, pushing away with the drink cart.

Rocking up and back, photos of Holly and Jim and Joey and Carol and Ariel in his lap, Noah whispers a prayer of thanks. "Never," he begins, "not Holly, not any of them. Not one wife, not one woman, not one child. Wherever it is I'm going, I'm married, I'm married still, and I'm staying married to every one of them," he vows. "No divorces. Life can divorce me if it likes, and Holly too, but I'm not divorcing anyone."

Noah tries to pray. His mind goes blank. He summons up the only prayers he can remember, those wedding blessings he heard the rabbis give voice to:

> Blessed are You, Unnamable G-d,
> source of the universe,
> Who purify us with Your commandments
> and give us marriage as a path to You.
> Blessed are You, Unnamable G-d,
> Who give us the mystery of marriage.
> Blessed are You, Unnamable G-d,
> source of the universe,
> Who created all things in Your glory...

Creaking, losing altitude, the 747 bounces in the night sky.

Flipping through his envelope of photos, Noah pulls out a publicity shot of Holly, an old glossy.

The photo winks at him.

"It's okay. You did the best you knew, Noah. I still care for you, honey, I really do."

"What if I don't make it? What about Joey and Ariel? What about Jim and Carol?" Noah asks.

"They'll survive," says Holly. "They'll get over it. It's okay," she says, reassuring him. "You're like Huck Finn setting out for new territory. Westward Ho, and all that."

"Ahem, let me have your attention. This is the Captain speaking. We'll be touching down at JFK in a few minutes. Check again to see that your seatbelts are fastened. Remove your eyeglasses, if you're wearing them, and prepare for a rough landing. We've enjoyed having you on board Flight 007 and, on behalf of our flight attendants and crew, I'd like to thank you for flying Bi-Coastal..."

Again Noah kisses the photo.

"What a romantic!" she says.

"All I know is I love you."

"Come off it. You're speaking in clichés," Holly laughs.

"You once told me you loved clichés. 'Clichés express old truths, the best kind,' you said, and you were right. Holly, what's wrong with committing to someone and staying with that person? Is there an alternative?"

"You know what the alternative is, Noah."

"Yeah, living alone."

"You know, working in soaps, you see a lot of comings and goings."

"I understand. Marriages are disposable, right? Families, husbands, wives, all disposable. Children are throw-aways."

"And our staying married is going to make a difference?" Holly cries.

"Yeah, it would make a difference. I'll tell you something, those vows we took, *in sickness and in health...for richer or poorer...*those vows are what I plan to go out saying.

"Come on, Holly, what do you say? *Forgive and forget. Live and let live. I'll scratch your back if you scratch mine.*"

"Well, you've got to admit, it's hard to do," she laughs, "you know, keep a marriage going."

"I'm not giving up, Holly."

"You don't need to convince me. Anyway, first things first. For starters, how about surviving the plane wreck, if there is one? Then we'll have something to talk about. Oh, and Noah, darling, if you do get to the next world, look under your pillow. I left another note for you."

—END

PRINTED AND BOUND
IN BOUCHERVILLE, QUEBEC, CANADA,
BY MARC VEILLEUX INC.
IN MAY, 1996